THE DRAGON'S FIND

Tahoe Dragon Mates

Book 6

JESSIE DONOVAN

Mythical Lake Press, LLC

The Dragon's Find
Copyright © 2023 Laura Hoak-Kagey
Mythical Lake Press, LLC
First Print Edition

Cover Art by Laura Hoak-Kagey of Mythical Lake Design
ISBN: 978-1944776695

Also by Jessie Donovan

The Dragon Family (LHD #5)

The Dragon's Discovery (LHD #6)

The Dragon's Pursuit (LHD #7)

The Dragon Collective (LHD #8)

The Dragon's Chance (LHD # 9)

The Dragon's Memory (LHD #10)

The Dragon Recruit / Iris & Antony (LHD #11, TBD)

Stonefire Dragons

Sacrificed to the Dragon (SD #1)

Seducing the Dragon (SD #2)

Revealing the Dragons (SD #3)

Healed by the Dragon (SD #4)

Reawakening the Dragon (SD #5)

Loved by the Dragon (SD #6)

Surrendering to the Dragon (SD #7)

Cured by the Dragon (SD #8)

Aiding the Dragon (SD #9)

Finding the Dragon (SD #10)

Craved by the Dragon (SD #11)

Persuading the Dragon (SD #12)

Treasured by the Dragon (SD #13)

Trusting the Dragon (SD #14)

Taught by the Dragon / Bronx & Percy (SD #15, May 18, 2023)

Stonefire Dragons Shorts

Meeting the Humans (SDS #1)

The Dragon Camp (SDS #2)

The Dragon Play (SDS #3)

Dragon's First Christmas (SDS #4)

Stonefire Dragons Universe

Winning Skyhunter (SDU #1)

Transforming Snowridge (SDU #2)

Finding Dragon's Court (SDU #3)

Tahoe Dragon Mates

The Dragon's Choice (TDM #1)

The Dragon's Need (TDM #2)

The Dragon's Bidder (TDM #3)

The Dragon's Charge (TDM #4)

The Dragon's Weakness (TDM #5)

The Dragon's Find (TDM #6)

The Dragon's Surprise / Dr. Kyle Baker & Alexis (TDM #7 / TBD)

Asylums for Magical Threats

Blaze of Secrets (AMT #1)

Frozen Desires (AMT #2)

Shadow of Temptation (AMT #3)

Flare of Promise (AMT #4)

Cascade Shifters

Convincing the Cougar (CS #0.5)

WRITING AS LIZZIE ENGLAND

(Super sexy contemporary novellas)

Her Fantasy

Chapter One

Jennifer "Jenny" Hartmann didn't know if she should scream, cry, or maybe do a little of both.

Pounding the heels of her hands against the steering wheel, she muttered, "How could you do this to me, after all we'd been through?"

As if her twenty-year-old car could hear and reply.

True, she knew it needed to go to a mechanic. A little red light had gone on about three weeks ago. However, ever since she'd been laid off from her teaching job last year and had been forced to move in with her sister, she hadn't had money for much of anything, and certainly not for fixing her car.

And yes, she shouldn't have attempted the mountain when it was cold, about to snow, and had a POS car to boot.

But when her brother-in-law's family had offered their mountain cabin to Jenny for a week, to give her time to think about what to do with her life and finally stop wallowing, she hadn't been able to pass it up.

Not even her sister's usual sarcasm about her car being such a great off-road vehicle had changed her mind.

Nope, Jenny had wanted—needed—to have some peace and quiet. Mostly, she wanted to stop thinking about her money troubles, about her asshat ex-boyfriend, or how she couldn't find a job doing the thing she loved.

So she'd chanced it with her car—ol' Bess, the name her stepdad had used for it before giving it to her on her nineteenth birthday—and had lost the roll of the dice.

Looking down, she checked her phone again. But nothing had changed—there weren't any bars, and the battery was dangerously low.

Oh, and yes, she'd forgotten her charger too.

When did I become this scatterbrained?

She knew the answer, but wasn't going to head down that road again. Her ex, Corey, could kiss her ass.

Scanning the surroundings, she ignored the falling snow and hoped for a side road, or sign, or anything to tell her she was near some kind of civilization.

Otherwise, she'd have to stay in her car and not freeze to death until someone else risked the icy roads.

Shivering, she sighed and tossed her useless phone into the passenger's seat. *Think, Jenny, there has to be something you can do besides sit here and become a human popsicle.*

There *was* a tourist town along this road, although she didn't know how far away it was. If it wasn't snowing and the sun wasn't an hour away from setting, she might've walked and chanced it.

However, not only would it be dark and cold soon, a dragon clan lived somewhere on this mountain.

While she didn't exactly fear dragon-shifters, she knew some didn't like humans. And a few stories said they kidnapped humans and kept them as wives and breeders, or something like that.

Given all the stories, she wondered why anyone applied to the Tahoe Dragon Mate lottery thing she sometimes heard about.

As Jenny zipped up her coat all the way to her chin, she sighed and stared out at the snow-covered landscape of pine trees. She would have to chance walking along the road. She might still freeze to death, but at last she'd be doing something and not just sitting on her ass, waiting to die.

Why didn't she live somewhere warm, like Arizona?

Gathering up her purse, phone—just in case she found reception before it lost power—and as many warm clothes from her suitcase as she could put on, she headed up the road.

Snow fell harder with each passing minute and her heart raced, her cold palms somehow still sweaty. Would she really die this way? Alone, frozen, penniless, and forgotten by everyone, by even her sister and her family?

Stop it, Jenny. Dark thoughts wouldn't help her. Although as she slowly trudged up the mountain road, every sound, every movement, every flash of color, made her more and more wary. Given her luck, she'd end up kidnapped or murdered.

Unwilling to give up, Jenny trudged onward, her

arms wrapped around her body, determined to find that little town and get warm again.

DANIEL TORRES PUT his hands into his jacket pockets as he walked, keeping an eye out for tracks, broken branches, or any sort of clue to the trespassers who'd breached his clan's outer perimeter.

Usually, he was quicker about locating someone, but the heavy snowfall—growing thicker by the moment—made everything a fucking slog. At this rate, he'd have to return to his cabin with nothing, and stay another few days at the edges of Clan MirrorPeak's territory.

His inner dragon—the second personality inside his head—spoke up. *It won't be that bad. It's not like we have much waiting for us back home.*

Don't start this up again, dragon. I'm not itching to suddenly find my mate.

His beast huffed. *We're thirty-five years old, and it's high time to look for her. Or, at least, find a female to kiss and fuck more than once a year.*

Daniel grunted. *Maybe we'll go to Tahoe and find a willing human. But only* after *we find the latest trespassers. AHOL has been bolder lately, and I won't risk the clan.*

AHOL stood for America for Humans Only League. They were assholes who wanted to kick all dragon-shifters out of the US and create a human utopia, or some such bullshit.

For years, the clans in the great Tahoe area had largely ignored them. However, in recent years, their attacks had grown bolder, bigger, and more dangerous.

As such, his clan took intrusions more seriously these days. And since Daniel was the best tracker in the clan, he spent a lot of time at the isolated cabin on the edges of MirrorPeak. It usually didn't bother him, but his dragon didn't like his mostly celibate life.

But Daniel had grown tired of sleeping with females who would mean nothing to him the next day. He'd always been the type of male who wanted their true mate or no one. And so he'd never dated, only fucked, and had put off looking for the female who might be his best chance at happiness. His job was too important to get distracted, especially with all the heightened AHOL threats.

His dragon huffed. *That's just an excuse. At this rate, you'll never find her. So once we get this latest threat done, you're going to make more of an effort. I'd do it myself, but I tend to scare people when I take control.*

When his inner beast took over their mind in their human form, he growled a lot, barked orders, and didn't have any of the subtlety his human half used. Even if the dragon halves attempted to talk less and smile more, it usually terrified humans.

Daniel wished it didn't because when he was finally ready to find her, to fit his mate into his life, he would've gladly handed over the mate-finding to his dragon.

With a sigh, he took out his cell phone and checked the time. He could search for another half hour before he needed to head back to check in with his clan. Cell reception was spotty as hell out here. Yes, he had a satellite phone but kept it back at the cabin—they were expensive as fuck, and he didn't want to risk dropping it in a snowbank.

He trudged through the trees until eventually he heard a female shout, "Of course I'd fall and scrape my knee. This is the shittiest day of all time, I swear. Fuck my life."

Frowning, Daniel changed direction and headed toward the voice. As she continued to mutter to herself, he finally reached the edge of the trees, next to the main road, and stopped a second to survey the area.

Struggling to stand in the middle of the icy road was a female. She was short and curvy, with shoulder-length hair that was…jagged? And as her scent drifted toward him, he knew she was human.

As she slipped on the ice and fell on her ass again, his dragon growled, *Go help her.*

How do you know she's not an enemy? It could be a trick.

Maybe. But if she keeps slipping on the ice, she could break her neck. And if she's innocent, do you want that on your conscience?

His dragon was right, he couldn't let the fool human kill herself. If she were innocent, it'd be a good deed, which might buy some bonus points with the American Department of Dragon Affairs. But if she were an enemy? Well, he'd find out and interrogate the shit out of her.

The plus side was his isolated cabin had nothing to tie it back to MirrorPeak beyond him and his phone.

Which he would guard with his life.

Removing his hands from his coat pockets, Daniel walked onto the road. The human saw him, gasped, and tried to scoot back, away from him. "Please, please, just leave me alone. I'm broke, have no money, and I'm so cold that touching my skin would turn you to ice. Really, I'm not worth it. I'll just keep going and I won't say anything about seeing you."

Daniel frowned. "What the hell are you talking about?"

And yet she continued to scoot backward, no doubt getting even wetter and colder. "I-I just want to reach the town."

He stopped walking toward her, and his dragon said, *We are sort of intimidating to strangers. Try being nice to her.*

The human gasped. "You're a dragon-shifter!"

He sighed. "Yes, thanks for letting me know, just in case I forgot after all these decades."

Some of the fear left her gaze, but not all. She drawled, "I understand sarcasm like a second language, thanks to my sister. There's no need for it." She clamped a hand over her mouth. And while a human probably couldn't decipher her next whisper, dragon-shifters had supersensitive hearing and he could. "I shouldn't have said that. He'll ransom me now."

"Oh, for fuck's sake." He put his hands up, showing he had nothing in them. "I'm not going to kill you, or ransom you, or do more than try to help you. Although if you keep being overly dramatic, I might just turn around, walk away, and let you freeze to death."

He wouldn't, but she didn't know that. If he could get her to be reasonable, everything would be fine.

Of course, reasonable was asking too much,

especially as she narrowed her eyes and growled, "I'm not being overly dramatic. Try being a woman out on an empty road, in the dark, alone. Add in my crappy life lately, and it's almost inevitable you'll cut me into pieces and bury me in the backyard. Maybe plant a rosebush or something, as a kind of trophy. Isn't that what serial killers do?"

His dragon chuckled. *She's kind of funny, in an unintentional way.*

No, she's being ridiculous.

Not giving his beast the chance to reply, he said, "Look—you can either calm down and tell me what happened, or I can turn and walk away, leaving you to the bears."

Her eyes widened. "There are bears out here?"

They hibernated in the winter, but she must be from out of town if she didn't know that. "Yes. No wolves, sadly, as that would've been a more dramatic end for you, which you'd no doubt like."

She narrowed her eyes. "Now, listen here, Mr. Dragonman. This has been the worst day of my life, maybe ever. My last year has been crappy—I lost my job, had an asshole ex who only stayed with me when I could support him financially, and I'm stuck living with my sister. And now? Now, I'm going to freeze to death in the middle of the road and probably end up a human popsicle treat for bears, or some other wildlife."

And then she burst into tears.

Daniel blinked, trying to decide what to do. Crying females was a weakness of his, for sure, and yet this one was a little bit crazy and he wasn't sure his usual methods of calming a person down would work.

Even so, he took a step toward her and tried to think of what he could do without making it all exponentially worse.

Chapter Two

Jenny could count on one hand the number of times she'd cried in public. She didn't like to show that kind of weakness to the world and usually saved it for the safe space of her bedroom.

But at the dragonman's prodding and his jibs at her being a drama queen, combined with her aching leg and how damn cold she was, it'd just been all too much.

And so now she sobbed in the middle of the road, in front of a complete stranger, and couldn't seem to stop.

She sort of noticed the tall dragon-shifter inch closer, but was too far gone to really care. If he was going to kill her, or rape her, or whatever, it wasn't as if she could stop it. She'd banged her knee when she'd fallen, couldn't seem to stand again, and didn't have so much as a pencil to try stabbing him in the eye.

Or whatever seemed to work in movies.

Before she knew it, the dragon-shifter crouched

down in front of her and gently touched her shoulder. She flinched, but he said softly, "It's okay. I think you just need to warm up and get something to eat. I have a cabin nearby. Say the word, and I can carry you there."

She focused on getting a grip of herself until her sobs became mere sniffles, and she fished out a tissue to wipe her nose. "I-I shouldn't."

"Well, maybe not. Especially if you think I'm a murderer, then you'd be walking into the lion's den. Or, should I say, dragon's den?"

She searched his dark brown eyes, his pupils flashing to slits and back. Weirdly, instead of fear, the action helped calm her a little. "Was that supposed to be funny?"

He shrugged. "Maybe."

He smiled at her, and it transformed his entire face from foreboding to drop-dead gorgeous. She finally took in his features—the dragonman had medium brown skin, black hair, and deep brown eyes.

Add in his muscles and height, and this guy took it to a whole new level of sexy.

It seemed the rumors about how dragon-shifters were too good-looking for their own good were true.

Shaking her head, she pushed aside her attraction —she was honest enough to admit she thought him hot AF—and tried to be rational. Well, as rational as she could be on this crappy-ass day. "Why do you want to help me?"

He didn't smile, or wink, or be overly charming. No, he grunted. "Because you're hurt, and it's my job to help those who need it."

Jenny racked her brain, trying to recall what she

knew about dragons and their clan structures. True, teachers taught a little bit about dragon-shifters in school, but mostly in high school. Since she'd been an elementary school teacher, her lessons had mostly been about legends, or dragon colors, or other basic stuff.

As if reading her mind, he added, "I'm a Protector for Clan MirrorPeak. My job is basically a type of security guard, but better. I've seen some human movies, and I most definitely don't fumble around and let villains go for stupid reasons, like falling for a sob story."

For the first time all day, she smiled. "What, too-small uniforms or clumsy movements aren't part of your job requirements?"

"No way in hell. I wear what I want in my human form. In dragon form, I don't wear anything at all."

Her cheeks heated. For a split second, she wondered what Mr. Sexy Security Guard looked like under all those layers.

Stop it, Jenny. Attraction had led her to Corey and a whole slew of bad choices. She'd keep her libido in check this time around, if it killed her.

He spoke again. "At any rate, it's too cold to strip and shift right now, not to mention impractical. I'd slip on the ice and never get into the air. However, my boots have traction and if you give the word, I can carry you to my cabin and help you. I promise not to cut you into little pieces and feed you to the bears."

Him joking about being a murderer oddly made her feel better.

Which was probably stupid, but what other choice did she have, really? No car, no reception, a hurt leg, and she couldn't even remember what it felt like to be warm.

She could either try to trudge along until she finally collapsed and froze to death, or risk it with the dragonman.

There was only one decision. Still, she wanted to ask one more thing. "Do you have a working phone? Maybe a landline?"

He shook his head, and her stomach dropped. Then he answered, "No, but I have a satellite phone you can use back at the cabin."

She sat up straight. "Really? That's the first piece of good news today. Hell, maybe in the last year."

As he stared at her funnily, Jenny realized she was doing it again—talking with no kind of filter. While she'd learned to keep herself in check inside the classroom, she'd sucked at it outside of it. Most people didn't like to hear about your shitty life out of the blue.

But she needed to try with this guy. Until she learned more about the dragon-shifter, she didn't want to give away too many details. Although her first name was common, so she blurted, "I'm Jennifer. Or Jenny. Just please don't call me Jen."

Crap. Why did she have to offer so many choices? She really, really needed to get her mouth under control.

The dragonman asked, "Why not Jen?"

Because Corey had called her Jen. Or, rather, "Jen, baby." Not that she'd tell him. "I don't like it."

He shrugged. "I don't care. Jenny is shorter than Jennifer, so I'll use that. I'm Daniel."

"Can I call you Danny?"

He growled, "No."

At the sight of his flashing dragon eyes, she put up her hands. "Okay, okay, Daniel it is." She put out a hand. "Nice to meet you."

It probably wasn't the smartest move, being all nice with a stranger, but she was so cold that her brain wasn't at its finest.

To her surprise, he shook, kept a hold of her hand, and stood. He gently tugged her upward, and she stumbled against the dragonman's solid, broad chest.

Leaning against him, she met his gaze and sucked in a breath. This close, his eyes were devastating, mesmerizing, and add in whatever he smelled like—man and something else—and she wanted to stand on her tiptoes and kiss him.

What the hell? She looked away. If she could stand on her own, she would've put distance between them.

But no, the dragonman merely tightened his grip on her hips and said, "Are you okay?"

Not really. She'd been about to kiss a complete stranger.

Apparently, she'd learned nothing from her past.

She cleared her throat. "My leg hurts a little."

"Then let me carry you."

Before she could protest, he swung her up into his arms and she had no choice but to wrap her arms around his neck. And for a split second, she cursed the scarf between her hands and his skin.

Although that scarf was probably a lifesaver because if she touched his warm skin, she might moan.

Willing her cheeks not to flush, she said, "Thank you."

He grunted and then carried her into the trees. The deeper they went, the more her fear should've grown. However, oddly, she felt more at ease and melted more against him, to the point she battled to keep her eyes open.

"Don't fall asleep."

At his commanding tone, she blinked her eyes a few times. "You sound like a military commander, or something."

"I've done my time in the Air Force. However, some dragon-shifters naturally have more dominance than others. I'm at the top of the scale, so it's just there."

Of course, he'd be a super alpha male, or whatever. At least he was nice so far and hadn't put her down just to look badass or superior. That kind of thing had never really floated her boat. Especially given her ex's criticisms over the years.

Damn Corey, intruding on her thoughts again.

As the silence dragged on, Jenny tried to think of what to say to the dragonman. Normally, she couldn't stop talking—one of her many faults—but she was so cold, so very cold, and it was all she could focus on.

Shivering, she nestled more against Daniel. His grip tightened around her body. Or maybe she'd imagined it. But as soon as he said, "There's the cabin," she sighed in relief. If she spent too much more time in his big, muscled arms, she might do something very, very stupid. Like touch the late-day stubble growing on his jaw, or trace his firm lips, or even lean in to breathe more of eau de dragonman.

Jenny only hoped she could contact someone to pick her up ASAP and get away from him quickly.

Otherwise, she might do something rash and get herself in trouble. The laws surrounding humans and dragon-shifters were complex, and she didn't even want to figure out the intricacies of them.

No, call her sister, get a ride, and go back home to figure out her life. That was her goal, and nothing else.

But to make a memory—because how often would she be in the arms of a dragon-shifter?—she did secretly inhale his spicy male scent and sigh. No man had ever smelled so good before. So much so, she wanted to just stay in his arms forever.

Yep, she was definitely in big trouble already.

DANIEL HAD REVELED in the warm, soft bundle in his arms the entire walk to the cabin. Most dragon-shifters were tall and lean, but the human was shorter and softer in all the right places. He kept trying not to think of her naked. Or to not imagine how he'd explore every curve and valley before finally parting her thighs to taste her and make her forget all about her bad day.

His dragon spoke up. *Yes, I like that idea. I want her naked and under us. Fast. Given how she's sniffing us, I think she's up for it.*

He'd noticed that too, as well as how she'd snuggled more against him during the walk. It was strange, as he'd rescued people before—he also worked with the human authorities sometimes when someone fell or got lost on the mountainside—but holding them, or even carrying them, had been nothing more than his next task.

And yet, with Jenny, he didn't want to let go.

Which was fucking ridiculous. He'd just met her. Not only was she a little dramatic for his tastes, she was also human. And his clan didn't have much luck with them, after all. Their last chance to pick humans from the Tahoe Mate Lottery had resulted in both humans leaving; the female giving up her baby and the male fucking the dragonwoman until she was pregnant and fleeing.

He'd heard about how it'd been better for Clan PineRock, and their humans had stayed. Not only that, they were happy and in love.

Not that he was thinking of love, or having a mate, or any of that nonsense.

His dragon huffed. *Why not? Maybe she's ours. She smells good, feels right, and would make life interesting. All you have to do is kiss her to find out.*

Right, and then start a mate-claim frenzy if she's our true mate. Which would make us crazy to have her, and she'd have to knock us unconscious and run.

Mate-claim frenzies meant he'd want to fuck her until she was pregnant. And if she didn't want it? She'd have to flee, and he'd have to suffer a year or more of pain and confinement, until his dragon finally calmed down.

And Daniel wouldn't let his clan down like that.

He reached the porch and took a second glance at the front porch light. It wasn't dark yet, but he'd left it on, just in case. Either the bulb had burned out, or the electricity had gone out.

It happened a lot at this remote cabin, but he hoped not this time. He didn't like the idea of Jenny cold and shivering, him unable to help her.

He unlocked the door and went inside. While definitely warmer than outside, it was colder than it should be. He flicked on the light switch, but nothing. Daniel cursed.

Jenny spoke up. "That didn't sound good. What's wrong?"

"Well, it seems your bad day isn't getting much better—the power's out."

She sighed and laid her head against his chest. He rather liked her warm weight there, but he focused on her reply. "Sounds about right. At this rate, the place will burn down and I'll die one way or the other today."

He threaded every bit of dominance he possessed into his voice. "No, you won't."

She looked up at him, searching his gaze. "Why do I feel like I should believe you?"

"Because I've spent my life living on this mountain and I know how to survive it."

"Maybe, but you're a dragon-shifter. Humans are a bit more delicate, I think."

His beast spoke up. *She's definitely delicate. I still say we should strip her and worship every inch of her body. If we make a roaring fire, she won't be cold.*

Fire, yes, but the rest—no way in hell.

Jenny's voice prevented his beast from replying, "What do you talk to your dragon about? That's what the flashing pupils mean, right?"

Well, at least she wasn't completely ignorant about dragon-shifters. "Yes to the flashing pupils. And no, my dragon isn't plotting to eat you, or anything."

His beast hummed. *I wouldn't mind eating her sweet pussy.*

At the thought of his face buried between Jenny's thighs, her fingers gripping his hair as she moaned, his cock stirred.

Banishing the thought—he wasn't about to get a hard on with Jenny in his arms—he moved toward the fireplace and set the human in the chair. He quickly tossed a blanket at her and crouched in front of the fireplace. A menial task would distract him from her soft sighs as she relaxed into the chair.

His dragon grunted. *Don't ignore her completely. I like her.*

After such a short time?

I just do.

Daniel's gut rolled. His dragon's early interest wasn't a good thing.

The responsible thing was to ask if Jenny was their true mate, but he kept that thought so tightly contained that his dragon wouldn't hear it as he worked on building a fire.

Although every small sigh and moan Jenny made as she melted into the chair made his cock harder.

Since he doubted he could call anyone to pick her up before morning—the roads were too treacherous—it was going to be a long fucking night.

Because he wasn't going to kiss her, if he could help it. He'd always dreamed of finding his true mate one day, but not yet.

And she most assuredly wouldn't be human.

Chapter Three

J enny covered herself with the blanket as much
as possible, loving how warm it was.

At least until the pins and needles started.

She bit her lip, willing them to pass. But as
they intensified, she cried out. Daniel was instantly in
front of her, his lovely eyes trained on hers. "What's
the matter? Is your leg hurt worse than you let on?"

Before she could answer, he flipped up the blanket
and gently took her leg. Despite the jean material
between his fingers and her skin, his touch sent a
tingle straight between her thighs.

One that most definitely had nothing to do with
the cold and warming up.

Daniel slowly ran his fingers around her calf, her
shin, and then to her knee, careful to never touch the
scrape visible through the ripped part of her pants.

Yet another thing the day had claimed—her
comfiest pair of jeans.

He murmured, "I need to clean your wound." He
met her eyes again. "Although nothing is broken, or

even sprained. It's mostly just the aftereffects of the cold."

For a beat, he merely stared at her, and she stared back. Not in an intimidating way, but more like how neither could move, as if they were opposite ends of a magnet.

Daniel finally released her leg and rushed into a room that, as best she could tell from her vantage point, was a bathroom.

Since he'd taken his coat off to build the fire, her gaze fell to his ass. A rather nice, firm one, by the looks of it. And as he strode back toward her, carrying some kind of first aid kit, she noticed how his muscled thighs strained against his jeans.

That's right—dragon-shifters were supposed to be mostly muscled, weren't they, from all the flying? Or something like that.

And even as he crouched down in front of her, she couldn't tear her gaze from his thighs. Oh, and she most definitely took a peek at his package too.

Nothing small there, either, she thought.

What am I doing? It wasn't as if she was going to have a one-night stand with a dragon-shifter. Hell, she knew nothing about him apart from his clan's name, his first name, and his job as some type of security guard.

Thankfully, Daniel's touch was mechanical as he cleaned her wound and put some antiseptic on it. Once done, he went back to the fire. Since the guy liked silence, and Jenny desperately wanted some conversation to distract her from the pins and needles —not to mention dirty thoughts about a certain dragonman—she blurted, "Why are you out here by yourself? I thought dragons lived with clans, in a kind of small town."

For a second, he said nothing. But finally he answered, "We do live in clans. But sometimes we have to monitor our borders, to keep the haters away."

Something from the recent news reports flickered in her brain. "You mean those AHOL people?"

He grunted. "Mostly." The fire roared. He turned to face her, crossed his arms over his chest, and asked, "Do you work for them?"

She blinked. "What?"

"Do you work for them? It would be completely plausible for them to use a distressed female to lower our guards, seeing as we'd help them."

For some reason, him thinking of her as some actress out to trap him made her angry. "No, I'm not some secret spy agent, or whatever the hell you're implying. I taught kindergarten for six years and am currently unemployed. It's why I have such a crappy car—I can't afford to fix it—and all I wanted was to stay at a family member's cabin, forget the world, and figure out what the hell to do in the future."

As soon as she finished, she nearly clapped a hand over her mouth. Why had she told him all that?

She fully expected him to inch away, or make excuses to go outside, or anything to get away from her. In Jenny's experience, revealing too much too soon to a guy was a huge no-no.

But Daniel merely studied her, as if trying to read her mind. But dragon-shifters couldn't do that, as best as she could tell.

Right?

Oh, how she wished she would've delved deeper

than the kid-friendly dragon lessons she'd done in the past.

He finally spoke, his deep voice making her shiver in a good way. "But why didn't you at least put chains on your car? It might've made it if you had."

She shrugged. "I didn't think the snow was that bad. And yes, I'll fully admit I didn't do my research. Not to mention I was a little distracted by…"

She shut her mouth. Nope, she wouldn't share even more personal information with him.

Except Daniel moved closer and leaned over until they were at eye level. "Distracted by what?"

This close, he was absolutely gorgeous. She'd always had a thing for brown eyes, not to mention his defined jaw and full lips. Maybe she should've entered one of those Tahoe mate lotteries when she'd had the chance.

He leaned even closer, until his face was only about a foot away from hers. "What distracted you to the point that you could've been killed?"

His words snapped her out of her lust haze. "I wouldn't have died. Probably." He raised an eyebrow, and she sighed. What the hell. It wasn't as if she'd see this guy again after she finally left. "My ex sent me his wedding invitation to some fancy, super expensive venue, okay?"

She remembered frowning at the letter, opening it, and then first cursing and then crying. Corey and her hadn't ended things on good terms, and he'd wanted to rub in how he'd found a rich lady to take care of him.

Now, all this time later, Jenny wanted to say fine— the other lady could have the asshole. But it'd only been four months since Corey had left her, six months since she'd lost her job, and her world had felt like it'd been closing in on her.

A light brush against her cheek brought her back to the present. She glanced at Daniel, his pupils flashing rapidly between round and slitted. She really shouldn't ask a dragon-shifter this—Jenny knew that much—but still she blurted, "What's your dragon saying?"

Daniel stood up, and she instantly missed his heat, his solid, comforting presence.

Wait, no, he couldn't be comforting. She'd just met him less than an hour ago.

The dragonman crossed his arms over his chest. "You really don't want to know. Although he and I agree you need to tell me that asshole's name. He could do with a lesson, and not the kind you would teach him."

As he smiled slowly, as if imagining the worst for Corey, she shook her head. "No way I'm doing that. It devastated me then, but I'm working on becoming indifferent. If someone won't stand by you at your worst, lowest moment, then fuck them. They aren't worth it."

Daniel shrugged. "Maybe. But he should still learn some manners."

At his petulant tone—as if he'd wanted to visit Corey and punch him more than anything—she laughed. "You can't just go around 'visiting' people to teach them a lesson, no matter how awful they are. It's harder for dragon-shifters since you're under way more scrutiny than I ever will be. That much I do know."

His smile vanished. "More than you know. And now, I need to check around the cabin and make sure it's safe. I won't be far, I promise." He moved to a desk, picked up some kind of phone, and came back. "This is a satellite phone. Use it to call someone who can help you. While I can get my clan's mechanic to come by as soon as it stops snowing, there might be someone else you want to come get you until the car's fixed."

Jenny took the phone. "There's someone in your clan who can fix ol' Bess?" At his blank look, she added, "That's my car."

The corner of his mouth kicked up. "You named your car ol' Bess?"

"Well, there's a story there. But I know you have things to do, so don't worry about it. I'm just grateful for your help, truly."

He grunted. "Okay, well, I'm going to scout the perimeter of the cabin. Don't go outside or try to leave. I'm faster anyway, and you won't make it far before I catch you."

Before she could say that sounded creepy as hell, Daniel was out the door and into the fading light.

Staring at the phone, she knew she'd call her sister, Jessica. But would it be to pick her up as soon as possible? Or just to let her know she was safe?

Which was crazy, of course. Jenny should want to get back to her family as soon as possible. And there was something about the dragonman, as if she could tell him anything and he'd listen. Maybe he'd offer solutions when she didn't want them, but it just showed how he didn't tune her out.

As she toyed with the phone, she wondered if the

dragonman's protective act was all a ruse to get her to talk. He probably thought she was still some kind of enemy.

So, yeah, staying with him was fucking stupid. She'd always been too trusting, wanting to believe the best in people.

However, Corey had been the last time she'd let that happen. Even if Daniel turned out to be the best boyfriend of the year—like he'd ever be hers, ha—she would be wary. It was just who she was now.

No matter how she hated it.

Sighing, she dialed her sister's number and as soon as Jessica picked up, she blurted, "My car died on the mountain and a dragon-shifter found me stranded."

Her sister, used to how Jenny would blurt things that didn't make sense to others, merely said, "Go back to the beginning and tell me everything. Well, after you let me know if you're okay. I told you not to drive up there tonight."

She resisted a snarky comment to her sister; Jessica only wanted to protect her, like she'd always done. Instead, she focused on her eventful day. "I'm fine. As for what happened…" She explained everything to her sister, even how the dragonman seemed to genuinely want to help her. However, she ended with, "But we both know where that got me before. So if you or your hubby could pick me up as soon as possible, that'd be great. I'll find out the coordinates as soon as Daniel gets back."

Her sister paused a second before saying, "Be cautious, but don't dismiss him outright. You should talk to him, learn more about the dragon-shifters, and see if what they say is true or not."

"What, exactly, am I supposed to find out?"

"I don't know, like if they have big cocks or not."

Jenny sputtered, "What?"

Her sister laughed. "I couldn't resist. But no, just find out what you can. My kids are asking more and more these days and I hate relying on hearsay. Maybe you can find out more. Oh! Idea! You could maybe help craft better dragon-shifter curriculums, or something."

She blinked. Usually, her sister was less random than her. "You came up with that from my one, random chance meeting?"

"Hey, I can't help it if I come up with awesome ideas."

"Right, like that time you thought we should try calling into school, make our voices sound older, and pretend to be Mom?"

Her sister snorted. "Well, it worked. The first time. We probably shouldn't have spent the day eating Mom's hidden candy stash under the bed. That's what got us."

Jenny smiled at the memory. "I miss her."

"I know, Jenny. Me too. And I'm pretty sure she'd support my idea. It's something that definitely needs to be updated from the 1970s, or whenever they last printed textbooks about dragon-shifters in the US."

"1982. But yes, forty years is sorely out of date." She bit her lip and added, "I'll think about it. For now, I'll work on getting directions and phone you back."

"And don't forget about a certain man's, ahem, package. Check it out too."

She growled, but Jessica laughed and hung up.

Sighing, Jenny put the phone down and rubbed

her forehead. Her sister's idea wasn't terrible. After all, the books used for older elementary school kids, as well as middle schoolers, were ancient.

But even if she embarked on the project, would any publisher want it? Could she survive a little longer without a job? She'd thought about substitute teaching, but it was erratic, and unreliable, and didn't pay super well. But maybe, just maybe, if she kept living with Jessica while she put out feelers for her textbook idea, substitute teaching could be enough to keep her from being destitute.

Besides, asking Daniel questions about dragon-shifters in general would distract her. Both from those gorgeous eyes and his package.

Because regardless of how nice or helpful Daniel was, Jenny wasn't ready to risk even just her body for a night of fun. She grew attached easily—another flaw that had allowed Corey to manipulate her—and she had to be careful.

So no touching, no wistful looks, and most definitely no getting naked with the dragonman. Words only, that would be her mantra. Anything else was off limits.

Chapter Four

Due to years of working for his clan's security, Daniel could do perimeter checks on autopilot. A good thing, too, because he kept thinking about the human female inside the cabin and what his dragon thought about her.

His beast spoke up. *Why are you ignoring me? I told you what I thought—we might finally have found our true mate. A touch helped, but only a kiss will tell us for sure.*

Daniel had barely had a second to enjoy the softness of Jenny's cheek before his dragon had demanded he kiss her.

Why now? Why her? If—and that was a big if—it were true, Daniel hadn't planned on looking for his true mate for at least a few years, until after the dragon clans in the greater Tahoe area had finalized some of their alliances.

Even if he wasn't clan leader, the MirrorPeak Protectors were all kept up-to-date on anything related to their home. Another dragon clan, PineRock, had started reaching out to MirrorPeak and others to propose meetings. Something that would've been unthinkable a few years ago, before PineRock's clan leader had mated an ADDA employee.

Daniel had met the ADDA employee—Ashley Swift—a few times in the past; the female was a force to be reckoned with. And given her drive, it truly was only a matter of time before the former isolation of the Tahoe clans would fade into memory.

As it was, all the dragons in the area had already agreed to help protect against AHOL. MirrorPeak's leader counted on Daniel's focus, his drive, his skills as a tracker and ability to find out information from some of the shadier human places in Lake Tahoe and other towns around the area.

A mate would screw all that up, and he could end up letting his clan down.

He finally replied to his dragon, *I can't risk a frenzy right now. Even if she is our true mate, our clan's safety is more important.*

Why can't we help the clan and claim our mate? It's not that hard to do both.

So you say. But if I have to worry about a mate, or a child coming, I'm not going to be able to focus on some of the more dangerous assignments.

His dragon huffed. *Let the younger, unattached Protectors have a turn. The world won't end if you delegate a little.*

Before he could reply to his beast, Daniel noticed a broken branch and went to inspect it.

The break was recent and on the ground were the faintest indents of footsteps; an hour later and the snow would've hidden them from sight.

Standing, he focused on the sights, sounds, and smells in the area. But beyond tree sap, rustling branches, or even a squirrel jumping from one tree to another, he heard nothing that screamed human.

But someone had been nearby. And for all he knew, someone had placed something dangerous inside the cabin during his absence.

Jenny. Turning, he dashed back toward the cabin. It still stood, the roof covered in snow, and light spilling from the windows.

At least the electricity was back on.

He surveyed the area, but didn't see any more footprints or signs of an intruder. Still, he needed to search the cabin straight away.

Barging inside, he found the main room that also served as a kitchen, empty. But as the sound of water came from the bathroom, his heart slowed a little. "Jenny? Where are you?"

"Just a moment!" came the reply from the bathroom.

Not wanting to alarm her if possible, he quickly looked under the sofa, the end tables, and even the dining table. He was just opening drawers in the kitchen to see if an explosive, or listening device, or anything foreign, had been placed when Jenny's voice filled his ears. "Are you a master chef or something? Because I'm going to be honest—I'm starving."

He turned, met her gaze, and then noticed her flushed cheeks. His dragon said, *She's not afraid of us like before. Talk to her. Calm her. Feed her. Then kiss her to see if she's ours, like I think she is.*

Ignoring his dragon, he closed the latest drawer and headed to the cupboards. "I don't keep much stocked here, but I won't let you go hungry." He rummaged around, and since it'd take time to cook, he found some chips and offered them. "Have a few while I make some grilled cheese."

She eyed the chips with wanting, but then shook her head. "I really shouldn't."

He frowned. "Why not? Are you allergic to potatoes or something?"

She snorted. "Most definitely not. I love them. A little too much."

Jenny crossed her arms over her chest, as if to guard herself, he didn't like it. He walked over, opened the bag, took a chip out, and placed it at her lips. "Eat it if you're hungry."

For a moment, she did nothing. Then she met his eyes and opened her mouth.

He placed the chip between her lips. She bit and chewed, making little moaning sounds of delight, and his cock hardened a little.

Fuck, what would it be like to have her lips around his dick? Or for him to take her plump bottom one between his teeth and tug?

His dragon hummed. *Yes, yes, try it. I want to taste her anywhere and everywhere. I want to see if she's ours.*

Ignoring his dragon, he took out another chip. But this time, Jenny took the bag and headed toward the couch. As she munched away, he forced himself to go back to the kitchen. He not only needed to make her something more substantial to eat, he also needed to ensure no one was listening in or would try to blow them up.

Some might think he was paranoid, but the League—the more common name for AHOL among dragon-shifters—was getting bolder and had tested some explosives in remote areas just outside his clan's lands.

Reminded of his duty to protect his people, Daniel quickly went about searching the rest of the kitchen, all while taking out bread, cheese, and butter. Only when he had the first sandwich in the pan did he realize how quiet it was. He turned, and there on the couch, Jenny slept on her side, her mouth open, fast asleep.

He smiled at her faint snores. Although his dragon, of course, had to ruin everything by saying, *See? She trusts us enough to sleep in our presence. With a little encouragement, she'll let us kiss her.*

That's not going to happen.

But as he watched her shift and nearly fall off the couch, he rushed to her side. He'd have to put her in his bed or she might hurt herself.

He gently picked her up, held her close, and watched to see if she'd waken. However, she merely snuggled into his chest and sighed before snoring again.

Holding her soft body in his arms, her heat pressed against him, he wondered what she'd look like naked. All her lovely curves ready for his hands, her nipples aching for his mouth, and her pussy wet and throbbing for his cock.

His dragon laughed. *You aren't going to be able to resist her for long.*

The comment allowed Daniel to banish any naked-Jenny thoughts, and he walked to the bedroom. *I'm not weak.*

Maybe not. But are you going to sleep on the floor? Or on

the couch? What if the electricity goes out again? She'll freeze unless we share the bed with her.

As Daniel laid Jenny on the bed and slowly pulled the covers over her, he replied to his beast, *I can keep her warm while also keeping my dick in my pants.*

So you are going to share the bed, then?

He brushed some hair off Jenny's face, and she murmured something unintelligible before falling slack again.

Even though she wasn't exactly a dignified sleeper —was there such a thing?—when asleep, her face was less tense, softer, and she looked younger. Although he had no idea what her age was, if she'd been teaching at least six years, she couldn't be too young.

One thing he couldn't argue was that she was so fucking beautiful. All her light brown hair fanned behind her—even if it was jagged, he'd have to ask about that—the curve of her cheek, her brow, just her entire face, made him want to wake up to it every day. After all, how much prettier would she be with the sunlight streaming in the morning? Or when he made her come and her eyes turned warm and satisfied?

His dragon laughed. *You won't last long.*

Daniel stepped away and exited the room. After shutting the door, he continued his search of the cabin.

And no matter how many times his dragon tried to goad him, he resisted. Because he didn't have time to find a mate right now. Plus, he barely knew her. Oh, he could fuck her easily, would probably never tire of her body, but her personality might drive him crazy long-term. Just because someone turned out to be a true mate didn't guarantee happiness. It was the best chance, but not failproof.

So Daniel focused on that aspect, especially about what would happen if she wanted to leave after a frenzy—provided she was his true mate—and how it could do more harm to his clan than good.

No matter what, he wouldn't let that happen. His clan was everything, and he'd protect them against any existing or potential threat, no matter what.

Chapter Five

Jenny woke up slowly, her first thought about how warm she was. Her sister always had the heat up way higher than she'd ever done— could afford, really—and it was a perk she'd definitely enjoyed.

However, something tightened around her waist and she opened her eyes. The room was small, with wood-paneled walls, and the window in the wrong place.

This wasn't her room at Jessica's house.

She tried to get up, but the band around her waist tightened and a deep, husky voice murmured, "Don't leave. You're so warm and soft."

Daniel. That's right, a dragon-shifter had rescued her.

Although why was she in bed with him? She didn't have a hangover, which meant she hadn't made a ginormous alcohol-hazed mistake, like sleeping with him.

He pulled her tighter against his front, his hard

chest meeting her back and a rather hard cock pressed against her ass.

Maybe she should be alarmed, but right here, right now, with his strong arm around her and his heat at her back, she felt…safe. Content.

Like this was home.

No, no, no. She wasn't that woman any longer, the one who trusted without a thought and fell for guys before she could blink.

She tried to get away again, and Daniel released her. As soon as she stood, the cold air made her shiver. Daniel growled, jumped out of bed—wearing only his sweat pants—and picked up the blanket from the bed. After wrapping it around her, he stated, "You should've waited until I built a fire again before getting up. The electricity has been going in and out all night, which is why I huddled with you to stay warm."

Looking anywhere but at him—because then she'd remember what it felt like to be held close against his warmth and her cheeks would turn red—she replied, "How convenient. And excuse me for panicking at waking up in a strange man's bed."

He narrowed his eyes. "I never would've hurt you, or worse."

She finally met his gaze. His flashing pupils didn't even faze her. "And how do I know that? I've known you for like, what, ten minutes? A guy I knew for years stabbed me in the back without blinking."

"Corey James."

She blinked. "How do you know that?"

"I looked into it last night, after you fell asleep. You won't have to worry about him anymore."

At his smug tone, her stomach rolled. "What did you do?"

"If I told you, I'd have to kill you." For a beat, she thought he was serious. Then he chuckled to himself. "You really are too easy to tease."

She narrowed her eyes, marched up to him, and poked his chest.

His very bare, hot, and muscled chest.

Ignoring that for the moment, she growled, "Don't push me this morning, Daniel. Or should I start calling you Danny to tease you back?"

He grabbed her hand and tugged until she fell against his chest. "Don't call me that."

Maybe she should struggle, or try to get away, but she couldn't seem to move. "Then be nice. I had a shitty day yesterday, I woke up in a weird place, I didn't eat dinner—potato chips don't count—and I'm sure my hair is a mess. Well, more than usual. You really, really don't want to push me right now."

He raised his brows. "How did your hair end up so uneven?"

She blinked at the non sequitur. "What?"

He lifted a hand, played with the ends on one side, and nodded his head toward her hair. "It's like you chopped away at it while wearing a blindfold."

With a growl, Jenny found the strength to push against him. Daniel released her, and she stormed to the bed, plopped down, and tightened the blanket around her shoulders. "You're a real charmer first thing in the morning, aren't you?"

He said nothing and since silence wasn't her best friend, Jenny sighed and explained, "I was trying to save some money, okay? So I cut it myself. Which, by the way, I don't recommend."

He ran a hand over his closely cut hair; it was as short as a Marine or some military guy. "I do my own."

She lifted a hand and raised her middle finger.

Daniel smiled. "Am I right to say you're not a morning person?"

The dragonman's smile disarmed her, and she scrambled to be cool and unaffected. "I used to be, out of necessity, when I was a teacher. But normally? No. Until I eat and have some tea, I'm the biggest grump on the planet."

Why had she said that, exactly? Damn it, at this rate, she'd spill all her secrets to this mysterious dragonman.

"I think I have some instant coffee, but probably not tea."

She scrunched her nose. "I can't have coffee or I turn into a nonstop chatterbox who can't keep still."

"How is that any different from normal?"

Jenny didn't care if he was a stranger, or could shift into a giant dragon. She picked up a pillow and threw it at him.

He caught it, of course, but it still made her feel a little better.

Daniel tossed the pillow onto the bed behind her. "Let me see what I can find. I also retrieved your suitcase from the car. It's over there." He pointed to the corner. "Once you're dressed, come to the kitchen and I'll have breakfast ready." His brows knitted together. "You aren't a vegetarian or vegan, are you?"

She scrunched her nose. "No way. I love bacon way too much."

"Good. Because bacon and eggs are what you're getting."

As he left—and of course as he walked out, she checked out his muscles and even glimpsed the dragon tattoo on one of his upper arms—she wondered how he'd retrieved her stuff. Had he really gone out in the cold and dark to get it for her?

And why did that do funny things to her heart? She'd never even dated a guy who'd been that considerate, and yet a stranger had done something so thoughtful.

Needing anything to distract her from thinking about the dragoman, Jenny went to the window, peeked out, and gasped. The snow was now as high as the bottom of the sill.

Which meant she wouldn't be going anywhere today.

The "before Corey" version of herself would've danced in place, excited for the chance to know the sexy dragonman a little better. However, her wounded self was a little jaded and almost resented having to spend time with him and risk making a huge mistake.

Because, despite every warning to be cautious, she kind of liked him.

And waking up in his bed, surrounded by his large, warm frame? Holy moly, that had been like heaven.

Remember to keep up your guard, Jenny. You can do this.

Right, she would, too. Especially since she wanted to talk to him and get to know his kind more, and maybe learn something to help with a textbook pitch idea.

Her idea might come to nothing, but she was going to take this opportunity to learn all she could about dragon-shifters.

Well, almost everything. She most definitely wouldn't be seeing a naked one any time soon, or learning if they really were as skilled in bed as the rumors said.

Although she probably already knew the answer to the latter question. Because, yeah, in her experience, men thought the clit was inside her vagina, or something.

Get your head out of the gutter. After taking a deep breath, she went to her luggage, picked out some clothes, and hesitated, eyeing the closed bedroom door. She shouldn't spy on Daniel, and yet, she wanted one last peek at him shirtless. To check out his tattoo, that's right. That was the reason.

She slowly opened the door a crack, grateful the hinges didn't squeak, and frowned at only being able to see his back. A nice back, with broad shoulders, but she wanted to see his arm.

Then he turned around, and she quickly shut the door. What were the chances he hadn't seen her peeking?

Probably zero.

Sighing, she went into the bathroom. Even though she'd taken a shower the night before, she treated herself to another one. And as the hot water cascaded over her body, she congratulated herself for recalling the still shirtless Daniel and not reaching between her legs.

Yep, she could resist him.

Really, she could.

As Daniel cooked the bacon and eggs, he slowly willed away his cockstand.

Damn, waking up with Jenny's warm, soft body in his arms had been the best thing in the world. He'd never woken that hard in the morning before, ever.

Although he had to admit, teasing her had been fun, too. He liked her quips, her tendency to ramble, and the way her hair stuck up every which way, as if deciding whether or not to follow the laws of gravity.

His dragon spoke up. *And yet, you still won't kiss her.*

Nor will I. Not only because she probably has no clue about what could happen, but also because I can't let my guard down with potential threats nearby.

Even if he hadn't found anything suspicious in the cabin during his search the night before, Daniel's instinct said there was a threat nearby. The waist-high snow would probably keep away any enemies, but the second it melted, they could attack.

And if he was in the middle of a mate-claim frenzy, where his dragon's sole goal was to impregnate their true mate, he'd be a sitting duck.

He'd fail his clan, himself, and his female.

No, he needed to figure out the threat and resist Jenny long enough to eradicate it.

His dragon hummed. *So you're open to kissing her once that's done, then?*

Nothing is set in stone. But if, and that's a big if, she's our true mate? I'd be willing to get to know her a little better.

Good. But don't take too long. If she leaves, we'll have to find her again.

Not wanting to have his dragon drive him to

becoming a stalker, he replied, *We have some time, so calm down.*

Mollified for now, his beast fell silent, curled up inside his mind, and fell asleep.

Ever since his inner dragon had spoken to him at age six and became active in his mind, Daniel barely thought about going from two voices in his head to one, so he slipped instantly into making breakfast. He had everything just about finished when the bedroom door opened.

He turned and sucked in a breath.

Even though Jenny merely wore jeans and a sweater, her cheeks were flushed pink from the hot water, her hair wet and dancing around her shoulders, and eyes bright, as if she'd found a better mood in the shower.

She smiled at him. "I definitely smell bacon. Tell me it's nearly ready because I'm starving."

As if on cue, her stomach rumbled.

And he didn't like it. The urge to take care of her, protect her, ensure she never went hungry, rushed through him.

Was it because she was his true mate, or just because he had a soft spot for saving people?

His sleepy dragon murmured, *Kiss her and find out.*

Ignoring his beast, he gestured toward the counter overhang and stools. "Sit down. It's nearly done, but I have some fruit you can munch on first."

She slid onto the stool, propped her elbows on the counter, and the front of her sweater draped open.

And of course Daniel looked down her shirt.

Her breasts weren't overly large, but he could fill

his palm with them. They were so plump and enticing. What color would her nipples be?

Jenny waved a hand. "Hello, my face is up here, Mr. Dragonman."

His eyes lingered a moment longer—deliberately —before meeting her brown-eyed gaze. "Why would you wear a low-cut sweater when it's cold out?"

She frowned. "Are you the fashion police? I didn't see that coming."

He growled. "You were shivering yesterday, and your lips were even a little blue, so excuse me for being concerned."

Grunting, he turned back toward the stove. He was being a bit of an asshole, but better to be that than do what he wanted—jump over the counter, haul Jenny into his arms, and kiss her as if he'd die without her.

Wait, had he really just thought that? Fuck, being around her was turning him into some pathetic romantic.

His dragon stirred, but Jenny spoke before his beast could say anything. "I never really thanked you for helping me yesterday. You could've just walked on and left me to fend for myself. But even though I'm human, you still came to my rescue. So, thank you, Daniel. I mean it."

Turning around slowly, his gaze met hers again. She was sincere—gone was the prickly female from earlier. He shrugged. "Maybe some dragon-shifters would've turned away at helping a human, but my clan doesn't. All the dragon clans in the Tahoe area assist with Search and Rescue operations, most of which are to help humans."

She propped her chin on her hand, the action pressing her breasts together and creating a delicious valley he wanted to nuzzle, and she replied, "I guess I never really thought about that. You never see it on the news, or online, or anything. It's usually the bad things you hear about dragons, or conspiracy theories about how dragon-shifters want to take over the world." He growled, but she put up a hand. "Hey, I'm not one of them. A friend of one of my old colleagues at the school mated a dragon-shifter. While I never had a chance to meet that woman—named Tori—once she moved onto Clan PineRock, by all accounts, she loved it there."

Daniel relaxed. He hated when humans based their opinions on lies and fear of the unknown. "Yes, I know the sister of Tori's dragon mate, a dragonwoman named Gaby. She helps with firefighting operations. It's a small world around here, so many of us know each other. Well, except for one clan. They keep to themselves, but don't cause any trouble."

Shit. Why had he even mentioned that? If the information got into the wrong hands, into some bastards in the League, it could mean bad news. An isolated dragon clan became an easy target.

Jenny tapped the counter with her fingers. "So even the dragons have differing alliances then."

"I guess you could say that." He dished out the bacon, eggs, and toast, determined to change the subject so he wouldn't let anything else slip.

Because even if he'd never had a problem keeping secrets in the past, something about Jenny made him want to share everything.

His dragon's lazy voice reverberated inside his mind. *You know why. I think I'm right about her, and she's ours.*

He ignored his beast and asked the human, "Why haven't you found another teaching job?"

She raised an eyebrow at the subject change, but thankfully answered, "It's tough. They want more kids in a classroom and fewer teachers. Plus, since I did some extra grad school classes after my Bachelor's, I earn more than a fresh-out-of-college teacher—teachers are paid more based on a combination of years taught and schooling—which they don't like."

His brows knitted together. "So they want to save money and hire less qualified teachers?"

She shrugged. "While not officially, it seems that way, at least in the district I worked in."

As she dug into her food—placing bacon on her toast, folding it, and eating it—he ignored her little moans of pleasure and said, "Our primary teacher in the clan is in his sixties. I doubt he'll retire until he can't physically do the job anymore."

Once she swallowed—which, bastard that he was, he watched her long, lovely throat the whole time—Jenny asked, "Do dragon-shifter teachers have universal textbooks or guidelines they all have to follow?"

"Why?"

She rolled her eyes. "I'm not after state secrets. I'm just curious. Teaching was a huge part of my life, so I'm interested."

Realizing how he was being a grumpy ass, Daniel decided to answer and help mollify her. "I'm not entirely sure. The last time I entered a classroom, I was seventeen. It's been a while."

"How long ago was that?" At his head shaking, she added, "Oh, come on. Give me some tiny detail about yourself. Don't think I haven't noticed how everything you talk about is related to the clan, or other dragons, or stuff like the electricity flickering. I don't even know your full name."

"Daniel Torres."

Deliberately remaining silent, he ate slowly until she finally huffed, "Tell me more than that. If the snow doesn't melt—and I doubt it'll happen today—then we'll be stuck in here together. Don't make me pull teeth the entire time, just to get a few words from you."

He pointed a fork at her. "I'll talk for as long as it takes for you to finish that plate. And no, don't make it last ten hours, either. I'm talking about a normal amount of time."

The corner of her mouth ticked up. "Do you have an official timetable, based on what's being served? Like, does pizza take ten minutes but meat, potatoes, and a veggie is twenty? Maybe two minutes for some water?"

His lips twitched. "No, but maybe I should. The Protectors like rules and regulations, and most of us learned how to follow them in the Air Force."

She made a deliberate show of eating a piece of bacon and Daniel nearly smiled. "All of us who want to be Protectors have to serve in the US Air Force first. And if there's ever a national invasion or attack, any of us could be called back to service."

"Really?"

He nodded. "Although that hasn't happened since World War II, when dragons had to help with Hawaii after the bombing of Pearl Harbor." He noticed her frown and added quickly, "The human history books don't mention that part. I don't know who made the decision, but little is said about how the dragons helped humans with past military campaigns." He shrugged. "But it doesn't matter. As long as we can keep learning the latest skills and technology during our stints in the military to use back on our clans, then they can decide whatever the fuck they want to share or hide."

She swallowed and leaned forward. "So do you have super secret spy gear, tailored specifically for dragon-shifters? Like, some sort of strap or harness that will stretch as you shift and never break?"

He chuckled. "Not really." Leaning forward, he dropped his voice dramatically. "Or do we?"

Jenny laughed, and the sound made both man and beast hum in approval. She hadn't really laughed since they'd met, and she deserved it.

Although where that thought had come from, he didn't know.

She said, "Well, I don't really care about spy gear. I would like to learn more about normal clan life, though. You see, I have this idea…"

When she didn't finish, he put down his fork and focused solely on her. "What idea?"

She bit her bottom lip, and it took everything he had not to move toward her and do the same with his own teeth. "Just promise not to laugh, okay? It's sort of a rough idea, and it may not come to anything, but I could really get into it. And given my lack of direction in recent months, it could change everything."

He studied her and noticed the uncertainty in her eyes.

Daniel didn't like it.

Rather than think about why, he asked, "What's your idea? As you said, we're trapped here for at least a little while. And it might help to talk about whatever it is and get some clarity. I know I do that with my job a lot."

And there he went again, sharing more of himself.

Jenny sat up tall. "Well…"

Her voice trailed off, but he merely waited. Daniel could be patient, and it was almost as if he wanted her to trust him enough to share this.

And damn, if he kept this up, he really might be in trouble.

His sleepy dragon said, *Just wait. If I made bets, I'd say you'd kiss her before the snow melts.*

Ignoring his beast, he waited for Jenny's answer.

Chapter Six

Jenny hadn't intended to mention her recent lightbulb moment, and yet, she had.

Although she hesitated to explain it. Daniel kept mentioning trouble with some humans, hinting at maybe even attacks, and she didn't want him to think she was a spy, like a honey trap.

As if she slept around with random men for information on a regular basis.

What am I thinking? Honey trap archetypes usually wore skimpy dresses, could flirt like it was a sport, and were always tall and graceful.

Most definitely not her.

Except...Daniel had stared down her sweater earlier, his gaze hot and hungry, making her feel as if she were desirable. Thank goodness she'd been bent forward, making it loose, so he couldn't see her nipples tighten under the fabric.

She'd imagined going over to him, pulling his head down, and kissing him. Which she couldn't do. Nope.

So she'd shoveled food to occupy herself. But now

her plate was empty, and she had nothing to really think about but Daniel.

So telling him about her idea was the best distraction. She wouldn't think of kissing him, or crawling into his lap, or even about how he'd carried her as if she weighed nothing the day before.

Clearing her throat, she finally answered him. "Well, you probably don't know this, but we do have textbooks about dragon-shifters. They change depending on the age—since I taught kindergarten, they were super basic and mostly stories—but no matter the grade level, they were all written decades ago. So, you see, I thought maybe I could try writing one myself. One that was more factual, up-to-date, and spent less time painting you all as evil villains, out to steal whatever you could."

He raised his brows. "Is that what they really teach?"

She nodded. "Mostly. The younger kids get to hear some of your legends, which is great. There are even a few new children's stories about dragon-shifters coming out from a UK publisher, supposedly written by humans living with a dragon clan. And I tried to use them when I could, but because of the state requirements, they couldn't be the main text." She tucked some hair behind her ear and eyed Daniel closely. "Are you sure you want to hear about this? It's not exactly exciting stuff."

He crossed his arms over his chest—damn, he had broad shoulders and had regrettably put on a shirt when she'd been in the shower—and nodded. "I might rescue humans occasionally, but I've never really sat down and talked with one at length. And since my niece wants to be a teacher eventually, this could be helpful for her. She's a little obsessed with humans, truth be told. She'd love you."

"Wait a second, back up—you have a niece? So that means a sibling as well? Or is it one of those honorary uncle deals?"

He shook his head. "I sometimes wonder about your thought processes."

Jenny's cheeks heated. "Not all of us can just grunt and glare all the time. I'm nearly a foot shorter than you, and it really wouldn't work that well."

Uncrossing his arms, Daniel leaned forward. "It wasn't a dig, I promise. I just don't think I've met someone like you before, is all. You're forthright and honest a lot sooner than anyone else."

She sighed. "I know. It's kind of a flaw of mine. But I'm the worst liar, and I really don't like wasting time by dancing around a topic. That was most definitely the hardest part of being a teacher—being diplomatic with parents about their children."

He snorted. "I bet." Propping his elbows on the counter, he leaned forward.

Damn, he hadn't even taken a shower or dressed properly and Daniel looked like a model or movie star with that chiseled jaw, deep-set eyes, and just the right amount of dark scruff on his face. The rumor about dragon-shifters winning the genetic lottery definitely seemed to be true.

Stop thinking about how sexy he is. Jenny cleared her throat. "I know I finished eating, but won't you tell me about this niece of yours? Who knows, maybe one day I could meet her and answer her questions."

Inwardly, Jenny groaned. She'd all but invited herself to his clan.

Daniel smiled. "That might happen, we'll see. As for my family,"—he paused, stood, and took her plate —"I'll tell you while I do the dishes."

She jumped up. "I'll help."

Once they were at the sink, standing close enough to one another, Jenny could feel the heat radiating from Daniel's body. He turned on the hot water and started talking again. "I have a younger brother. He has a mate, and together they have a son and a daughter. My niece is the youngest, and even if I'm not supposed to have a favorite, she is. I can't help it."

Jenny laughed. "I understand that. I have two nephews, and I love them both to pieces, but one always wants to see me, always lights up when I come into a room, and I can't help but have a favorite."

He glanced at her and then went back to washing dishes. "She's eight, and determined to be a teacher and change the world. Since I lived with humans for a year when I was with the Air Force, she always asks me how things are different for them. Although I don't claim to be an expert, or anything."

Just imagining Daniel patiently answering his niece's questions made her grin. "The doting uncle. That's super sweet."

He grunted. "I prefer nice. Dragonmen aren't sweet."

She laughed. "Denying it means it's totally true." Daniel growled, and she added, "Fine, fine, we'll say nice for now. But I still think it's sweet." She bumped her hip against his. "At least your ratio of growling to talking is improving."

He sighed, and she couldn't help but chuckle. He was so fun to tease.

Daniel finally started washing the dishes and handing them to her to dry as he went. He said, "But back to your idea—what, exactly, do you need to know?"

She shook her head. "I'm not sure yet. The idea is recent, and I need to do some research. Is there any internet here?"

He shook his head. "No, it's down and we haven't installed satellite internet out here."

"You know, you really are more tech-savvy than I expected for a dragon-shifter."

"I have to be, to protect my clan. That's why I'm out here in the first place."

He stilled, and she knew he regretted revealing that bit of information. But she wasn't going to let it go. If he thought she was some kind of spy, so be it. Who knew when she'd have the chance to ask a dragon so many questions? "What threats do you have to worry about?"

Daniel merely washed the plates and then the last pan. Only once she'd dried them off did he turn to face her and replied, "AHOL, mostly. You might know them better as the League."

She'd vaguely heard news reports about an attack here or there. "A little. Since everyone can basically record with their phones, some stuff ends up in the news sometimes."

"That's both good and bad, but mostly good. It means ADDA can't cover up everything like in the past."

It took her a second to equate ADDA with the

American Department of Dragon Affairs. "But didn't one of their employees mate a dragon-shifter somewhere near Lake Tahoe? I swore I heard that somewhere."

"Yes. Thanks to Ashley, we've had it better than most. But how a dragon clan is treated hugely depends on where you live."

Okay, that sentence alone made her think she could write an entire series of books about dragon-shifters in the US. "Let's focus on the greater Tahoe area for now. Do you have dragon clan gatherings? Special events? Do school children get together and get to know each other? Or does everyone remain isolated?"

They still faced each other in front of the sink, and Daniel searched her eyes, leaning closer in the process. A mixture of male spice and earth filled her nose, and she resisted leaning in for a better sniff.

He smelled good, though. And for a second, she wondered what it'd be like to press her nose to his neck, inhale, and then nip his skin.

Daniel's pupils flashed to slits and back again. His gravelly voice was low and rolled over her, making her shiver in a good way. "Don't do that."

"Do what?"

His pupils flashed even faster. "Dragons have super senses. Did you know that?"

"I think so. Why does that matter?"

Daniel moved to her ear, his hot breath dancing across her skin. "Because I can tell when you think dirty thoughts, Jenny. And it drives my dragon mad."

Her heart raced. And the longer Daniel stayed next to her ear, never retreating, the more heat rushed through her body and ended between her thighs.

Crap. Was that what he was talking about? He could smell her? So much for women being able to hide arousal easier than men. That didn't seem to be the case with dragon-shifters.

She should be embarrassed, but as he lightly caressed her upper arm, down to her hand, and back again, Jenny couldn't seem to care. "When you say mad, do you mean commit-murder-crazy or merely lust-crazy?"

He chuckled. "No holds barred, eh, Jenny?"

An apology formed on her lips—Corey had always told her to learn to think before speaking, and it was second nature—but Daniel placed his forefinger on her lips and leaned back until he could meet her gaze. "Don't look fucking embarrassed. I love how you speak about anything and everything. I've spent so many years having to do the opposite. And even if it was to protect my clan, or my country in the Air Force, I didn't always like it."

As they stared at one another, Jenny swayed a little toward Daniel. Just the feel of his finger against her lips, warm and rough, made her want to push his hand aside and kiss him.

Just as her body followed her mind, and she stood on her tiptoes to move closer to his face, panic flared in Daniel's eyes. He pushed her away and took three giant steps backward.

The action stung. Had she read all the signs wrong?

Daniel growled, and said, "Don't look like that."

"Like what?"

"Like I just stole away your kitten."

Anger flared at his words, and she forgot all about her embarrassment. "Well, excuse me. I didn't know I had to smile and laugh at being rejected. Good to know dragonmen aren't so different from human men—you both want us to smile more and make you feel better."

She turned to leave, but Daniel grabbed her wrist and said, "Don't leave. Not like this."

She should storm off, she really should. Months of reliving her last relationship had revealed just how much she'd taken from Corey, suffered his mean words and unrealistic expectations, and how she'd tried everything to please him.

There was no way in hell she'd do that again, if she could help it. Glancing over her shoulder, she barked, "Why the hell not? We may be trapped, but I can stay in the bedroom and give you space. Don't worry, I won't try kissing you again. Message received, loud and clear."

He growled, moved to right behind her, and he replied, "You have no fucking idea what I want, Jenny. But what I want and what I can have are two very different things."

She blinked. That wasn't what she'd expected him to say.

Still, she wasn't going to put up with his bullshit. As Jenny tried to turn around, Daniel wrapped an arm around her waist from behind, keeping her in place. She growled, "Explain yourself or let me go, Daniel."

With a sigh, he answered, "Okay, I will. The truth is—my dragon thinks you're my true mate. And if I kiss you, it'll cause a world of trouble. Mainly, I won't be able to protect you."

Her heart thumped, and she croaked, "Did you just say true mate?"

"Yes." He nuzzled the side of her neck and she willed herself to stay strong. "Do you know what that means?"

It was hard to concentrate with Daniel rubbing his face against her skin, back and forth, the slight stubble of his jaw sending waves of heat throughout her body. "Something about your dragon wanting to claim me, sex, and a baby? I think?"

He kissed the side of her neck, and she couldn't hold back a sigh. "Yes. If you are my true mate—and I won't know for certain until I kiss you—as soon as I press my lips to yours, my dragon will claw to take control. He'll want to fuck you over and over again, until eventually you're pregnant. And I can't let that happen."

Just when she'd thawed a bit toward him, he had to go and say that. "Talk about mixed signals. Even putting aside the fact you haven't asked me about if I'd want that future or not, why are you so against it? Because I'm human? Too chatty? Some other fault I need to lay bare before you give me any sort of answers?"

For a beat, he said nothing. And then another.

She willed herself to stay strong, to not go down the road of faults, of memories of her ex constantly pointing them out, that lead to crashing self-esteem.

When he still didn't say anything, she refused to cry at his rejection. Fine. He'd helped her, and she'd thank him. But if they were to stay in the same cabin for who knew how long, well, she'd keep her distance.

As she tried to walk forward, tugging at his arm around her waist to be let go, Daniel whispered, "You shouldn't be right for me in any way, and yet, being with you makes me feel like I've found my home. I just want to hold you and never let go. I know that sounds ridiculous after such a short time, and I probably should have my head checked, but there it is."

She sighed. "Nice to have a compliment paired with another backhanded criticism. Let me go, Daniel. Now."

"I'm not doing this right. Let me explain. Well, as much as I can."

"The truth, or nothing. I've dealt with lies before with my ex, and I won't accept them again. I know we're nothing, just two strangers, but I don't like feeling as if I'm not worth even some truths, Daniel. It hurts. A lot."

He hugged her tighter against him and murmured, "Then I'll tell you the truth. Just don't run away. At least, not yet."

The words piqued her curiosity long enough to wait a second to see if he'd explain himself.

Chapter Seven

Daniel knew he'd fucked up. Jenny had sounded on the verge of tears, and both man and beast hadn't liked it.

But he was in an impossible situation. Protecting his clan was everything, and no matter if Jenny was, in fact, his true mate, he'd known her less than a day. How was he supposed to explain the threats from the League, his entire reason for being stationed in this cabin in the first place?

His dragon spoke up. *Don't completely push her away. We should protect her, give her a chance, and share at least a little. Otherwise, she might not want anything to do with us. We'd lose our true mate.*

You can't know it for sure without kissing her.

I know. And you'd better not chase her away. Talk to her. Let her in.

His dragon flicked open his wings inside his mind, and he growled. *I'll try.*

Daniel held Jenny a minute, inhaled her addictive female scent from where her neck met her shoulder, and couldn't resist kissing her skin. She shivered a beat before stiffening. She said, "Start talking or I'm going to stomp on your toes and try elbowing you until you let me go."

Even if he doubted her ability to break his hold, he instead took a deep breath and blurted, "I'm here looking for enemies. If I kiss you and it does start the frenzy, it'll put you at risk. Not only that, it could put my entire clan at risk if my enemies capture me and try to ransom me." He laid his head on her shoulder. "I've wanted to kiss you since yesterday, Jenny. But too much is at stake. One burden of being a Protector for the clan is that you sometimes have to put your wants second, no matter how much you don't want to."

She relaxed a little, and he nearly sighed in relief. She might be softening toward him. "What enemy? Are we safe now? Why can't you just have some dragons fly in and watch the cabin?"

His heart thumped harder at the undertone of her words. "You want to risk a mate-claim frenzy?"

"I-I don't know. But I don't like you making the decision without me." She wiggled, rubbing against his cock, and he sucked in a breath. "Will you let me go so we can talk face-to-face? It's hard to concentrate when I'm surrounded by a hot, muscled dragonman."

His dragon snorted. *Just wait until she's naked. Then she'll be surrounded and stuffed full of dragonman.*

Stop it, dragon.

His beast laughed and then fell thankfully silent.

Daniel released Jenny, and she turned around. Unable to resist, he cupped her cheek and stroked his thumb against her soft skin. Her eyes searched his, and he let as much truth and desire show through as he could.

She gasped. "You really do want me, don't you?"

"Why do you sound so surprised?" She bit her bottom lip, and he narrowed his eyes. "This has to do with that dickhead ex, doesn't it?"

"Er, maybe."

"No matter what he said or did, he's a fool. Any male who took advantage of your sweetness and then tossed you aside when it became a little difficult isn't worth your time."

"How can you say all this? You've known me less than a day."

Lowering his head, he whispered, "Because it's the truth. I don't know if it's because we're probably true mates, but I think we've both been more forthright than we'd intended, given how we were strangers yesterday. Am I right?" She bobbed her head. "I think that's why I feel drawn to you and want to kiss you to see if you are mine. But it's going to take some time. Don't think I'm putting it off to string you along, or eventually reject you. No, it's because if I couldn't protect you and you were hurt, then I couldn't live with myself."

"Is it really that serious?"

His first instinct was to hold back. But he fought it, knowing he needed to prove he trusted Jenny a little. He'd never divulge his clan's biggest secrets this early, but anyone who paid attention to the area would know what he was about to say. "Yes. There have been more and more test explosions being set off in the forest around the clan. They've been careful to never set foot inside our land—which would've brought ADDA down on their heads—but the intimidation tactics have done their job; many inside the clan are worried about leaving it."

Her eyes widened. "I had no idea it was that bad."

Unable to resist, he cupped her face with both hands and lightly stroked her cheeks. Merely touching her calmed him and kept his usual anger about the League at bay. He nodded. "At first, ADDA took it seriously. But lately, things have become more lax. I don't have proof, but I believe a League sympathizer has either entered their ranks or bribed them to be less thorough about dragon-centered attacks."

"I wish I knew someone who could help you. But there is a long-term solution." She leaned forward a fraction, giving him hope. "I think some of the superstitions and hatred of dragon-shifters are because humans simply don't know that much about your kind. Even if it won't solve your immediate problem, I think education is key. And I'm not just saying that because I was a teacher."

He loved being able to see the flecks of gold in her brown eyes. "I'm sure the teacher part of you will always be there, and that's a good thing. And you're right—it won't help in the present, but I think your earlier idea of new textbooks could help in the long run. Once I can find the current culprits and get them arrested, I'll help you with your project, Jenny. I promise."

She smiled up at him, and his heart skipped a beat. Before she could say a word, he blurted, "You're so beautiful, Jenny. I can't believe you dropped into my life, or that you're most likely my true mate."

"Well, technically, it's my crappy car's fault I'm

here. And I had no say in being a true mate. But maybe, I think, I'd like to get to know you better. Then I can decide what to do." She bit her lip and added, "I just wish I could kiss you without possibly triggering a sex marathon. You can tell a lot from a kiss."

He gently brushed some hair off her face. "There are lots of kisses that don't require my lips to touch yours." He lowered his head and brushed his lips against her neck. "Like here." Then he went lower to kiss at the base of her throat, lingering to lightly lick her skin. "Or here." He moved his head to between her breasts and kissed over her clothes. "And here."

Her voice was breathless as she asked, "And lower?"

He glanced up to meet her gaze. "Do you want me to? Because if I could strip your jeans and kiss you where you ache most, then I could probably go at least a few hours without thinking of claiming your mouth with my own."

Her breath hitched. "You actually want to lick between my thighs?"

The incredulity in his voice made him frown. "Of course I do. Just imagining how you'd taste, your scent, and your sweet moans as you convulse around my fingers makes my cock hard and aching for you."

Her cheeks heated, and she glanced away. "I've only had a man do that twice, and only because I pushed."

His inner dragon growled. *Who the fuck was this ex of hers? Eating pussy is delicious, and amazing, and makes a female scream.*

I don't know, but I have a feeling he pummeled her self-esteem, and it still affects her.

His beast huffed. *Then help prop it up and convince her we'd eat her pussy for hours and still not be satisfied.*

Daniel stood, took her chin gently in his fingers, and made her look at him. "I crave to know your taste, Jenny. Not only that, but watching you lose yourself to pleasure will make both man and beast hum in satisfaction; dragon-shifters take pleasing their mates seriously. Especially if you're mine, you'll come from my semen anyway. So eating your pussy until you come is a way for me to prove I'm worthy of you."

She raised an eyebrow. "You can't be serious. Men don't talk like that."

He leaned down, until his face was mere inches from hers. "Maybe humans don't, but I assure you, dragon-shifters do. And if you don't believe me, you can ask any of my clan members when you visit."

"When I visit? So it's decided already?"

Her smile softened her words, and he leaned down to nip her jaw. "Well, you need your car fixed, right? The closest people who can do that are Clan MirrorPeak."

She laughed. "Okay, okay, so that's a valid point. I thought you were going to say you'd toss me over your shoulder and carry me off."

Daniel leaned back. "If you want that, I'll do it. Just imagining your soft breasts against my back, your lovely ass right there for me to squeeze and grip, and your scent invading my nostrils—you have no idea how hard that makes me, Jenny. I almost want to beg."

She lightly swatted his chest. "Don't be ridiculous."

"Do you want a demonstration?"

At his serious tone, she squeezed. "You're not making crap up, are you?"

"No."

Her breathing quickened and her cheeks flushed. "So is that how you'll get me to the bed before you strip me and lick between my thighs?"

He'd noticed how she kept her words almost PG-rated, probably because she'd been a kindergarten teacher. And the devil in him wanted to hear her say the R-rated versions.

Moving to her ear, he placed a possessive hand on her ass and squeezed. "Eat your pussy? Yes. Ask me for what you want, exactly, Jenny. I'm a grown male, and telling me you want that, or to fuck you with my mouth, or to make you come hard, will make me harder than I've ever been in my life."

She breathed, "Daniel."

Taking her earlobe between his teeth, he tugged. He loved how she moaned and leaned against him. Once he released her flesh, he added, "Say it, Jenny. Tell me exactly what you want and I'll make sure you orgasm so hard, you'll forget your name for a few seconds."

"I…" Her voice trailed off, but then she cleared her throat and whispered, "I want you to eat my pussy, Daniel. Make me come. Please."

Her "please" snapped something inside him. He might not be able to fuck her with his cock, but he sure as hell was going to do it with his mouth and erase any previous half-assed memories she had of her ex.

Stepping back, he tossed her over his shoulder and

strode toward the bedroom. He made sure to grip her ass cheek, massage it, and lightly slap her.

"Daniel."

"Daniel good or Daniel bad?"

He did it again, and she moaned. "Good, definitely good."

His dragon hummed. *Yes, yes. We can at least do this, although I still say you should just kiss her and claim her. That way, no one else can have her.*

I won't let anyone steal her away from us. Ever. But I can't think only with my cock. Would you risk her safety?

No.

Then we do this my way.

They reached the bed, and he gently removed Jenny from his shoulder and sat her down. Placing an arm on either side of her hips, he leaned close. "Do you want me to remove your jeans slowly or quickly?"

She squirmed on the bed, and the scent of her arousal made his dragon hum. Somehow, Daniel made himself focus on her reply. "Fast. Definitely fast."

"Even if it means they'll be in pieces?"

Her eyes widened, but she still nodded.

With a growl, he extended a talon. With one deft swipe down her leg, and then the other, he could easily tug them off and tossed the ruined garment over his shoulder. "Spread those lovely thighs for me, Jenny. Let me see you before I do the same to your underwear."

A less patient male would've shredded the sensible cotton panties too. But he wanted her dripping, and aching, and sometimes a little anticipation made it all that much better.

Something his teenage self hadn't learned, but he was a grown-ass male now. And he knew what to do.

Jenny slowly spread her legs and rubbed her hands on her thighs. She was so soft everywhere, and he couldn't wait to have her curves cradle his hips as he thrust into her. Or to nuzzle his whiskers over her inner thighs and lightly mark her.

And even with her still wearing panties, he could see how she drenched the material.

"Daniel?"

Her voice snapped him back to the present, and he kneeled between her thighs. Meeting her gaze, he nearly growled at the uncertainty. "You're fucking beautiful, Jenny. I could stare all day and still not get enough."

She murmured, "You don't have to say fancy words."

"Your ex was an asshole."

"What?"

He rubbed one hand over her left thigh and then the right, taking his time to caress, and squeeze, and lightly score his nails over her sensitive flesh. "Forget him. Your body makes me so hard it hurts, Jenny. You're perfect, and I'm going to prove just how fucking desirable you are."

Leaning down, he nipped her inner thigh with his teeth.

"Oh," she breathed.

He did the same to the other, and then slowly kissed her thigh, up to where it met her hip, and then the material of her panties over her pussy. He inhaled deeply and growled, "Your scent drives me fucking crazy, Jenny. I want to taste you so badly. But not until you understand just what you do to me."

He hadn't intended to kiss every inch of her body, except for her mouth. But her uncertain look still ate at him, and he wouldn't have that.

Time to treasure her, as any male should.

Daniel kissed her belly just above her panties, then slowly, oh so slowly, pushed up her sweater and undershirt, exposing her soft, pale skin.

He pressed his mouth to her skin just above her navel, then up a little further, until he stopped just below her bra. Pushing her shirt all the way up to her neck, he stared at her breasts and growled, "I need to suck them, and nibble them until you writhe and beg for me to finally touch your pussy."

"Yes, please."

Maybe if he wasn't so distracted by her beautiful body, he'd smile at her politeness.

But no, he extended a talon and sliced off her bra, exposing her breasts.

Fuck, she had pink nipples, all beaded and begging for him to suckle.

He took one into his mouth and lightly bit her as he tweaked her other one with his fingers. She laid her hand against his head and pressed, almost as if she were afraid he'd leave.

Not fucking likely.

He suckled deep and then twirled her hard nipple with his tongue. Releasing her, he blew across her wet flesh slowly and she dug her nails into his scalp. "Yes, Daniel. More, give me more."

She was so fucking responsive to his touch, and both male and beast wished they could just fuck her now and claim her. He'd never tire of learning what she liked, giving it to her, and making her senseless by the time she screamed his name.

His dragon growled. *Stop dawdling. I want to taste her pussy. Now.*

Almost. I can't neglect the other one.

Before his beast could reply, he sucked her other nipple into his mouth, giving it the same nips and licks and suckles as the first. Jenny had placed her feet on the bed and used them to push her lower half against him.

Fuck. What he wouldn't give to sink home and feel her come around his cock.

Since he couldn't do that, he released her nipple and kissed his way back down, taking time to press his lips to as much of her skin as he could. When he reached her panties, he took the hem and then ripped them down the side.

After tossing them away, he pressed her thighs wide and stared at her wet, swollen pussy. "So fucking perfect. And mine."

Without another word, he lowered his head and licked her slowly, from her entrance up to her clit and back again.

Her taste was addictive, and he lapped at her pussy, loving how she wriggled with each stroke of his tongue.

"Daniel, please."

Looking up, he saw her dilated pupils and flushed face. "Please, what?"

"Make me come." She arched her hips a little upward. "I'm so close already. Please don't stop."

He placed his hands under her ass and tilted her up, to better feast on her flesh. He did lap a few more times at her entrance, unable to resist another taste, before he finally moved his tongue to her clit.

He circled around her slowly, learning what she liked—fast, with lots of pressure. Then he plunged two fingers into her hot pussy and he groaned. She was so tight, and he loved how her inner muscles instantly gripped his fingers.

His cock throbbed, wanting to plunge into her, but he kept his focus on her clit. As he slowly thrust into her pussy with his fingers, he finally suckled her hard bud, and she arched as she cried out. Her inner spasms went on and on, her cries doing the same, until her body finally calmed down and she relaxed against the bed.

Daniel raised his head, met her eyes, and licked his fingers clean.

Fuck, her orgasm was delicious.

His dragon hummed. *You should do more, much more. Fuck her, kiss her, make her ours.*

Since his inner beast lacked the demanding, urgent tone that supposedly accompanied a frenzy, he didn't panic. As far as Daniel knew, his dragon should behave as long as he didn't kiss Jenny's mouth.

Crawling up her body, Daniel finally settled next to her and kissed the side of her neck. "How was that?"

"Amazing. I'm still trying to catch my breath."

He chuckled as he gripped one of her breasts possessively. "It should be like that every time. Although I'm a little competitive, so next time I want to make you scream even louder."

"Next time?"

He lifted his head and cupped her cheek. "Of

course next time. Now that I've tasted you? Damn, I'm going to want to do it again and again."

She frowned. "Are all dragon-shifters like this?"

He grinned. "Most are. We know how to treat our partners."

Although, as he said it, Daniel mentally cursed. He didn't want to scare her off, and all but saying she was his this early might do that.

Still, he stroked her cheek and waited for her answer. He wouldn't brush it off because to him, she was his already. Yes, they still didn't know every little detail about each other. However, he knew enough, combined with his dragon's instinct, to know she was his best chance at a happy future.

Chapter Eight

Jenny was still trying to make her brain work when Daniel mentioned pleasing their partners. Did he really think like that already? It was crazy, and probably her post-orgasm brain wasn't entirely rational, but she wanted to believe him.

She'd never had a man who'd been so gentle yet possessive, or had ever focused on her coming instead of him.

Not to mention his kisses and caresses made her feel beautiful in a way she'd never really had before.

He didn't even seem to mind the post-breakup weight she'd gained from eating cookies and ice cream. If anything, he'd worshiped her as if he'd never seen such a beautiful woman before.

Oh, she so wanted to believe the fantasy and how everything would be perfect. But the cynical part of herself wouldn't accept it. "Why are you so confident about us?"

He'd never stopped stroking her cheek, and she almost purred at his firm yet warm touch. He replied,

"I learned a long time ago to trust my gut. It saved my ass in the Air Force a few times, and even more since coming back to my clan and being a Protector. And my gut says you're the future, Jenny. I know you're human and the whole true mates thing might be too much to believe at first. But it means a lot to dragon-shifters. It's not full-proof, and sometimes it can go wrong, but more often than not, it's so amazing and wonderful that those of us who haven't found our true mate get jealous."

She searched his gaze, wondering what it'd be like to be so certain of gut feelings. She'd never had much luck with them in the past. "Well, I'm open to dating you, Daniel. And I'm definitely on board with doing whatever sexy stuff we can without kissing to start the frenzy. But I'll need some time for anything more than that."

"Because of the ex asshole." She nodded, and he sighed. "Now I wish I'd broken his legs, or something like that."

"You still haven't told me what you did while I was asleep."

He shrugged. "I asked one of the tech-savvy members of my clan to find something on his computer or phone to embarrass him."

She shouldn't want such a petty thing to happen to Corey, and yet she couldn't help but ask, "And did the clan member find anything?"

He smirked. "Plenty. It seems your ex has been cheating on his new bride already, and she received some of the proof earlier today. I expect he's in for a rough time."

"Considering how I later found out he cheated on

me with the woman he married, I'm not surprised. But she has all the money, so hopefully she can make his life hellish by withholding it."

"So you're not going to lecture me?"

Jenny shook her head. "I should, but I won't. I never had a way to even remotely hurt Corey like he hurt me. Not only for his betrayal once I lost my job, and he declared he only wanted a woman who could support him, but also his little nitpicks about my appearance or actions." She bit her lip a second, still unsure why she was sharing all this. But she'd come this far, so she added softly, "They built up over time and made me doubt myself."

He growled and lowered his face closer to hers. "I should pay him a visit."

She placed a hand on his jaw. "Don't. He's not worth it any longer. Besides, you're a dragon-shifter and you'd get into a lot of trouble if he reports you. And then where would we be?"

Daniel's pupils flashed, and then he grunted. "Maybe. But if I ever see him, I'll find a way to teach him a lesson, no matter what."

She smiled. "I've never had someone want to protect me before. Well, apart from my sister and parents. But never a boyfriend."

He ran a hand down her side until he gripped her hip possessively. "You'd better get used to it. Dragon-shifters are very protective of what's theirs."

As she stared into Daniel's eyes, she didn't feel alarmed or worried about things moving quickly. Her gut said he would do as he said and always protect her.

And it was something she'd never known she'd

wanted before. But the thought of someone always having her back—someone that wasn't her sister—made her chest swell with warm fuzzies.

Even though she wasn't usually bold when it came to sex, she decided to try it. Running a hand down his chest, his hip, and then to his cock, she gripped his hard length through his sweatpants and squeezed gently. Danial groaned, and she said, "I want to do for you what you just did for me."

His pupils flashed even faster than before. His husky voice rolled over her. "Are you sure? I didn't make you orgasm expecting anything in return."

"And that's exactly why I want to suck your cock and make you come, too."

As the words left her mouth, her entire body heated. She'd never thought to say such things. And yet, she found she rather enjoyed being blunt and to the point in this area of her life, too.

And judging by how Daniel's cock grew even bigger in her hand, he liked it.

She desperately wanted to please him, so she pushed against his shoulder until he lay back on the bed. "I don't have talons, so I have to do this the slow way."

He growled. "As long as you have your hands on my body, that's all I care about."

A sense of power rushed through her, and she ran a hand under his shirt. At the first feel of his hard, warm skin, she groaned.

Up, up, up, she trailed her fingers until she found the small nubs of his nipples. She pinched one, and he bucked his hips, his cock twitching in her grip. "Fuck, Jenny. Do that again."

She did, and Daniel was even louder.

Needing to see his skin, she removed her hands and pushed his shirt up until he took it the last bit and tugged it off. With all his light brown, smooth skin on display, she licked her lips. It was her turn to taste.

Leaning down, she kissed his breastbone, and then as many places on his chest as she could. The combination of warm flesh and spicy male scent made wetness rush between her legs.

She kissed down, down, until she reached the waistband of his sweatpants. Lightly running a finger under the waistband, Daniel groaned. "You're going to kill me, aren't you?"

Smiling, she met his gaze. "I hope not."

He licked his lips. "Just thinking of your hot mouth sucking my cock has me so hard, Jenny."

Eager to see what would probably belong to her one day, Jenny tugged down his sweatpants until his dick sprung free. It laid heavy against his belly, thick and huge.

She squeezed her thighs together, just imagining all that man inside her.

No, not a man. A dragonman. She was learning the difference.

A difference she was coming to think was too good to be true.

No. She wouldn't ruin this with doubts, so she pushed them aside and took his cock in her hand.

He was so hot, and she stroked him once, circling the tip with her thumb, and loved finding a drop of precum there.

He really did want her, her touch, just her.

Holding on to that fantasy—she really couldn't

believe otherwise for now, not yet—she lifted his cock, lowered her head, and blew.

Daniel bucked his hips and growled. A quick peek showed his pupils flashing quickly. For a second, she froze. "Is your dragon out of control?"

His voice sounded strangled to her eyes. "No. Just suck me, Jenny, and it'll help."

Since her mouth watered just thinking of taking him into her mouth, she finally placed his cock between her lips and lowered her head.

Daniel's hand went to her hair, and he cupped the back of her skull. No pushing, or forcing her down. No, he just held her and waited for her to do things at her own pace.

Even now, when his dragon had to be screaming for her to move, he was holding back.

Maybe Daniel really was different from her ex and other men in general.

Tired of others invading her thoughts, she focused on the dragonman under her. She bobbed her head, using her hand to help stroke his length, and used his moans, groans, and when he dug his nails into her scalp to judge what he liked.

Which was fast, and a little rough, and especially when she took him as far as she could without gagging.

Soon she lost herself to the rhythm, enjoying his taste and scent, and the simple fact he trusted her enough to let her do this. Because, really, if she were out to get him, she could clamp down on his cock with her teeth and have him at her mercy.

But she never wanted to do that. No, Daniel was already revealing parts of herself she'd lost during her last relationship, and she couldn't imagine what a future might look like.

However, it was one she wanted to explore.

Soon he bucked his hips and then stilled her head with his hands. "Stop, Jenny. I'm going to come."

The thought of tasting her dragonman made her pussy even wetter. She batted his hands away and increased her pace, laving him with her tongue before sucking him as deep as she could; she even lightly nibbled here and there.

He finally cried out and hot jets filled her mouth, over and over again, and she swallowed him down.

When Daniel finally stilled, he whispered, "That was fucking amazing," and she smiled around his cock.

After one last slow lick up his length, she licked her lips and crawled up to him. He gently brushed some hair behind her ear. "I'm going to dream about that mouth constantly, Jenny. Fuck, I've never come that hard before."

A thrill shot through her. "Good."

He laughed. "Someone's starting to sound like a possessive dragon-shifter."

She smiled. "Well, you must be rubbing off on me."

He kissed her cheek and then moved to the far side of the bed. "Come here."

She obeyed, and once he had her cradled in his arms, with her head lying on his chest, he kissed her brow. "Sleep. Because next time, I'm going to tease you a little more and keep you on the edge. It'll make the fall that much harder."

As she snuggled against his hard, warm body, she thought, *I'm already falling, which scares me.*

Cocooned against her dragonman, Jenny soon fell asleep with a smile on her face, her dreams full of a future that maybe she could have after all.

Chapter Nine

A loud boom instantly woke Daniel. He sat upright and scanned the room. No one was there, but he heard some sort of roaring fire not that far away.

Fuck, fuck, fuck. Had someone attacked?

Jenny blinked up sleepily at him and he said, "Get dressed, Jenny, and be ready to run."

His words banished the sleepiness from her gaze. "What?"

He jumped out of bed. "Just do as I say. There was an explosion and I need to see where. But if it was caused by the League, we'll need to flee. Quickly."

He'd threaded dominance into his voice, and it worked on her. She nodded. "Okay. Shout if you need me. But Daniel? Promise me you'll be careful."

It was strange having someone care so much about him—his friends and family did, of course, but it felt different coming from Jenny—and he nodded. "I will. Now, hurry and be ready."

He hated leaving her behind, and especially alone.

But there was only one window in the bedroom and he'd had bars installed on it years ago. It was the only way he could sleep if out in the open without the protection of his clan, like with this cabin.

It should help keep Jenny safe now, too.

His dragon spoke up. *I don't hear anyone inside the house. But the fire is close.*

Yes, and I wonder how the hell they managed it in the waist-high snow.

When hate is involved, anything could happen.

His dragon fell silent, knowing Daniel needed to concentrate without distractions. A quick sweep of the house revealed nothing out of the ordinary. Since he'd tugged on some clothes while doing the sweep, he quickly donned his boots and coat and peeked out the window near the door.

The light was faint, the sun already setting at this time of year. However, in the distance, an orange glow signaled some kind of huge inferno.

No doubt his clan had heard it, but he dialed his boss on the satellite phone. The head Protector, Axel, picked up on the first ring. "Is it near you?"

"Yes, it's not far from here. I'm on my way to investigate. But I'm going to need help transporting the human here with me to safety."

Since he'd shared helping her in a report earlier, his boss didn't ask questions. Instead, Axel grunted. "The snow is too deep to send any kind of vehicle. Not even the snowmobiles will work in the darkness, at least not with a fragile human. We'll have to retrieve her by dragonwing. Are you sure we can trust her?"

Because if a human reported to ADDA about

them carrying her to their clan, it could land his clan in a hell of a lot of trouble.

But he knew Jenny wouldn't betray him like that. "Yes, we can. Although she might need someone there to calm her on the ride. It can't be me because I know this area the best and need to be on hand."

"I'll send Solana."

Solana was his boss's mate. She was only half-human, but that still might help when it came to explaining things to Jenny. "Good. How quickly can you get here? I can't leave her unprotected, but I also don't want anyone getting away."

"Eli is already in the air and should arrive any second. I'll have my mate and their transport there in about ten minutes, along with a few more Protectors to help you. Call me again if you hear or need anything."

The phone line went dead, and he pocketed the phone. He itched to go searching through the woods, but he wouldn't leave Jenny.

He'd just made it back to the cabin when a green dragon landed in the clearing near the cabin—purposely kept open to allow dragons to come and go —and touched down. Once his friend Eli finished changing back into his human form, he strode forward. "What do you know?"

He shook his head. "Not much."

"Daniel?"

Jenny's voice came from the doorway. Her gaze darted to Eli—a very naked Eli—and Daniel instantly stepped in front of him. True, dragon-shifters didn't think of nudity as much as humans did, but he didn't want his future mate seeing anyone's cock but his, if he could help it. "We're going to get you out of here while I and the others search the area. It's not safe for you here."

Her gaze darted over his shoulder and Daniel saw his friend wave at his human. He growled, "Don't flirt."

"What? I was just being friendly."

Daniel moved his gaze back to Jenny and lightly touched her cheek. "My boss's mate is coming so she can ride back with you. The only way to get you out of here with all this snow is to fly by dragonwing. They'll carry a basket for you to ride in."

Jenny blinked. "They do that?"

He leaned in close and whispered, "Usually not. But I won't have you stuck here and possibly put in danger. Just promise not to mention it to ADDA, okay? It's a rule violation, and we'll be punished."

She frowned. "Of course I won't say anything." She touched his cheek, and he wanted to lean into it. "But will you be okay by yourself?"

"I'm not going alone. More help is arriving."

Eli's voice behind him shouted, "And I'm here already. I'm one of the best, little human. I'll have Daniel's back."

He growled and tossed back, "Don't call her little human. Her name is Jenny."

Jenny placed a hand on Daniel's chest, garnering his attention again. "It's fine. I'm more concerned about you. I don't want you to get hurt. After all, we still have to try this whole dating thing to see if we fit."

He smiled, kissed her cheek, and murmured, "I'll find a way back to you, Jenny, no matter what."

She searched his gaze, and he radiated as much

confidence as possible. There was always risk, yes. But a well-trained dragonman wasn't easy to kill.

His human finally nodded. "Okay. Will everyone keep me updated, though? I don't think I can stand being in the dark."

Running the back of his fingers down her cheek, he replied, "I'll make sure of it. Now, quickly pack what you need and wait inside the cabin. The others should be here soon."

She looked at him for a few seconds, as if debating whether she should say something else or not. But in the end, she merely smiled and headed inside.

As soon as the door closed, Eli snorted. "When did that happen? Last I heard, you were going on and on about not being ready for a mate."

He grunted. "We don't have time for your teasing bullshit. Now, let me tell you about the surrounding land and the tracks I found recently. That way, we can have two parties approaching the explosion from different sides."

Even if Eli tended to joke and tease, when it came time to work, he became deadly serious.

Daniel had just finished sharing everything with his friend when a small group of dragons flew to just above the cabin and hovered in place. One by one, they descended into the small clearing, shifted, and dressed, until they all were in their human forms, the large carrying basket off to the side.

As Daniel explained the situation and headed out with the other Protectors, he looked back one last time at the cabin. He wanted to give Jenny a proper goodbye, but knew every second counted. They might already have lost the trail of those who'd set off the explosives.

And so he focused on finding those who might try to hurt his female. Because only once he vanquished that threat could he return to her and woo her to be his mate in truth.

Chapter Ten

Jenny paced the living room, tapping her hands against her thighs, wishing she could go outside and ask Daniel more questions.

However, she didn't want to distract him. And judging by the blaze and smoke she'd spotted from the front door, it wasn't some accidental, small explosion. No, even if she was a heavy sleeper and hadn't heard anything, it had to be huge.

A knock on the door made her jump. Taking deep breaths, she willed herself to calm the hell down. Dragon-shifters probably dealt with this kind of thing on a regular basis—given how quickly Daniel's clan had responded to send backup—and she could keep it together. The last thing they needed was another problem to deal with.

That's right, you can do this. Make a good impression on the dragon-shifters. Because if she and Daniel did go through with the mate-claim frenzy, she'd have to live with them.

Not wanting to think about how that would change her life, she raced to the door, looked through the peephole, and asked, "Who is it?"

"My name's Solana, from Clan MirrorPeak. We're here to take you to safety."

The light brown-skinned woman stared straight at her, as if she could see through the door, and her pupils flashed to slits and back.

She opened the door and tried not to stare. Most dragon-shifters were tall—male or female—and Solana was no different. She towered over Jenny, her frame lean and toned, judging from her biceps peeking out from her dress. Not to mention she was gorgeous, with dark brown eyes and long, black hair that didn't stick up every which way like Jenny's.

Yep, dragon-shifter genes were amazing things, really.

Although her mind remained stuck on the fact, the dragonwoman wore only a summer dress despite the snow. She blurted, "Aren't you freezing?"

Solana smiled. "A little, but my coat fell out of the bag I carried—I'm not the steadiest flier when I'm in a hurry. But I'll live. I just need to grab some blankets, and then we'll leave."

She strode inside while another dragon-shifter—a male—stood at the door. Since he remained silent and glared at her, Jenny focused on Solana. "Are you the one who'll carry me?"

"Oh, no way. I'm just here to keep you company." She patted her small, rounded belly, a detail Jenny had missed at first. "My mate would kill me if I tried to carry anything heavy while pregnant."

Jenny quickly picked up her coat and held it out. "It'll be big, but here, you take it. You need it more than me."

Solana paused for a second, and her smile turned warmer. "No, you keep it. I'll be fine with a few blankets, I promise. But thanks for offering. It shows you don't hate us, which is always a good start when you're the true mate of a dragon-shifter."

Still not quite ready to discuss that with strangers, Jenny cleared her throat. "I don't hate dragon-shifters. There's a ton I don't know, but I'm willing to learn. Especially since I have an idea, one I can share while we fly." Realizing she'd just assumed the dragonwoman wanted to hear her ramble, she quickly added, "If you want. I can be quiet, if that's easier."

Blankets tossed over her shoulders, Solana replied, "Of course I'd love to hear it. My mother was human, but died giving birth to me." Her gaze turned wistful. "I'm always curious about what humans think of us. After all, there haven't been any human mates on Clan MirrorPeak in a long, long time."

"I'm so sorry about your mother."

The dragonwoman placed a hand on her shoulder and squeezed. "It was a long time ago." She released Jenny and strode toward the door. "Now, come on. My mate placed you in my charge, and I need to see you delivered safely."

She blinked. "That makes me sound like a package."

Crap. There went her mouth, not listening to reason and her brain again. She needed to be grateful MirrorPeak wanted to help her despite the risk.

Before she could apologize, Solana waved a hand in dismissal. "You are, but dragons take fulfilling promises and vows pretty seriously, at least in my clan." She walked closer, her voice soft, "We'll protect you, no matter what, Jenny."

"And what about Daniel?"

She smiled. "He's one of the best of the best at what he does. And in the worst-case scenario—I'm a realist, to my mate's constant annoyance—we have our doctors and nurses at the ready. You'll soon see how the clan is one big family, and we do whatever it takes to help one another. Well, most of the time. My brother-in-law is super annoying sometimes. You met him earlier—Eli."

She'd barely made the connection—Jenny had a feeling she'd need a chart of who was related to who —when the dragonman at the door knocked and opened it. "We need to leave. The blaze spread to some of the trees. And while the snow is mostly keeping it contained, if it reaches the cabin, we'll be in big trouble."

At the thought of being trapped and burned alive, Jenny quickly tossed on her coat, grabbed her suitcase, and followed Solana out the door. They stopped in front of a large, hot-air balloon-type basket. The main difference was that it had a long, thick bar above it instead of a burner, and it was kept in place with other bars and chains.

Solana opened the little door and gestured with her hand for Jenny to go inside. "Get in. We'd better turn our backs while Chris changes. I know humans can be uncomfortable with naked strangers, for whatever reason."

She eyed the muscled dragonman—now shirtless —and had to drag her gaze away. "I wouldn't mind a peek, but I know Daniel wouldn't like it. And for now, I don't need to add to his worries."

Once they were secure inside the basket, Solana stared at her for a few beats before saying, "You're definitely not what I expected."

She raised her brows. "Do I want to know what you expected?"

Shrugging, Solana replied, "Humans are, generally speaking, afraid of us. There are some exceptions, of course, such as the America for All Alliance. But most are indifferent, want to study us, or hate us."

A dragon jumped into the air, and Jenny realized Chris had finished shifting. He deftly maneuvered down to grip the bar in his rear talons, and beat his wings until they ascended. They went higher and higher, until they were finally above the tree line.

As soon as Jenny looked down at the mountain and dense forest, she was grateful not to be afraid of heights. Otherwise, she'd miss out on the beautiful mix of green, white, and even dark patches of rock. "It's so pretty up here."

The basket jolted a beat before settling. Solana replied, "I wish I could enjoy it, but it's a little weird for me not to be the one flying and in control." She raised her voice. "Try to be a little more gentle, or I'm going to lose my stomach."

Chris's dragon form didn't respond, but the rest of the ride was a hell of a lot smoother.

Which she appreciated because the feel of the cool wind against her cheeks, combined with the beautiful lake and trees below her, was like something out of a dream.

Only when she saw the gathering of houses, shops, large, open areas—landing areas?—and even some dragons flying around the small town did she know they'd arrived at Clan MirrorPeak.

Which meant she'd have to meet the clan leader soon, like really soon. And given her luck, she'd blurt out something embarrassing.

She must've said something aloud because Solana chuckled. "Don't worry, my mate will also be there— he's in charge of all security—and Axel's used to all kinds of people." She winked. "Although he sometimes mumbles that I'm the worst of them all."

Jenny couldn't help but laugh. "You guys must be close, if you can joke about it."

A dreamy look crossed Solana's face. "He's my best friend, my partner, my everything." She met Jenny's eyes again. "And part of that strength comes from admitting faults to one another, and even teasing about them sometimes. It's fun to laugh with someone who knows you that well, loves you no matter what, and would die to protect you." She leaned closer. "You're about to get a crash course in dragonmen and how they treat their mates, Jenny. Prepare yourself, because it can be a bit much for outsiders. However, if you want a future with Daniel, you'll need to get used to it."

If she agreed to kiss Daniel and go through the frenzy.

But as they landed and a small group of people headed toward them—including a tall dragonman who only had eyes for Solana—Jenny took a few deep breaths and hoped she could make a good impression. Because regardless of how things panned out with Daniel, she wanted to get to know the dragon-shifters better, and maybe help the rest of the country do so too.

Chapter Eleven

Daniel moved quietly through the trees—well, as best he could, given the large amount of snow still on the ground that occasionally crunched under his feet—and ignored the ever-increasing heat. They were close now.

His dragon spoke up. *I still say we should scout the area from above first.*

Armando is doing that right now. We know these woods the best, and they're relying on us to look for any clues.

Because so far, they hadn't found any traces of who'd set the fire beyond a few snowshoe prints; ones that obscured any shoe size.

However, the stench of explosives had long ago told them it was a deliberate fire and not an accidental one.

The heat was almost unbearable when they finally reached the edge of the tree line, near a small clearing. At the far side, the blaze roared and tickled the nearby trees. A few were trying to catch, but the snow was helping to keep it from spreading rapidly, thank fuck.

He said to his beast, *Help me listen for anything unusual. If it's like their attacks in the past, they'll have someone nearby filming it to use in their next video.*

It was one of the eerier things the League did, especially when it included a victim burning to a crisp, which they'd captured previously. They were sick fuckers on so many levels.

His dragon growled. *They won't get one of us this time. ADDA allows us to defend ourselves, if it comes to it. And I plan to make it extra painful, if the opportunity arises.*

He wouldn't dissuade his dragon; the League had taken one of his clan members a few years ago, and everyone still grieved at the dragonman's loss.

Standing beyond the edge of the trees—which should keep him out of sight—he listened. The roar of the fire dominated everything, but the blaze had sent the animals scurrying already. There also wasn't any running water from nearby streams—they'd frozen—and no cars would be on the treacherous road about half a mile away.

He concentrated, using his training from both the Air Force and his years as a Protector to determine any subtle noises, ones that would give an enemy away. Since he hadn't heard from his other clan members yet via the satellite phone, set to vibrate, he couldn't move his position anyway.

One minute, then another. He could sense Eli nearby, but nothing else.

Snap. A branch broke about twenty feet away, to the left. Since none of his clan members should be there, it meant something—or someone—was.

Daniel moved quickly but silently, careful not to break any branches or cause any snow to tumble off the trees. It was tricky, given how thick the forest was here, but thankfully he'd patrolled them so many times over the last couple of weeks he could almost maneuver through them blindfolded.

When he was close to where the sound had originated, he paused and listened again. While no unusual sounds reached his ears, there was a faint scent of onions mixed with human.

His dragon grunted. *It has to be one of those bastards.*

Having heightened senses was both a blessing and a curse for dragon-shifters; bad breath became a whole awkward thing. At least in this case, his onion-loving target gave him away.

Daniel moved closer, closer, ever so much closer to the scent, until he heard some material or clothing rub against a tree or branch. Scanning the trees in the fast-fading light, he finally spotted the human male. He held up a phone, raising it higher, as if trying to catch more footage from the thicket of trees, one that blocked most of his view.

He wore a backpack, jacket, and a ski mask—all black.

His dragon huffed. *As if that will hide him from us. If anything, he's a dumbass as it makes him stand out against the snow.*

Hush. I need to approach him carefully.

In delicate situations like this, his beast had learned to follow his commands. Daniel debated what to do. He could take the guy down himself, but it might risk giving away his position if the asshole had friends in the area.

And yet if he waited for his teammates, this bastard might get away and Daniel risked losing him.

Because no matter how good a tracker he was, the snow played havoc with everything, and the human might find a way to escape.

As he debated what to do, he saw the man put his phone back into a pocket and took out a cylindrical black device that fit perfectly into his grip.

One that had a red button on the top.

The man smiled, watching as the dragons circled overhead.

Fuck. There were more explosives, who the hell knew where.

Before the man could place his thumb on the trigger, Daniel jumped and tackled him to the ground. He managed to push away the device, out of reach of them both, and wrestled with the man.

Despite his lean stature, the human was strong; desperation and hatred no doubt fueled him.

However, the human wasn't stronger than a dragon-shifter.

Before Daniel could restrain the man's hands, the human arched and put just enough space between them to reach into his pocket.

And in the next second, something exploded, and the world went black.

Chapter Twelve

Once the basket was on the ground and the dragon landed off to the side, Jenny took in the small group waiting several feet away. Solana pointed toward the tall, pale man with bright red hair. "That's my mate, Axel."

He smiled at Solana before he turned his assessing gaze on Jenny. She did her best to keep her head high, which earned a whispered, "Awesome, just like that," from Solana.

He strode forward, along with another tall man, except his skin was light brown and his hair black. Solana gestured toward him. "That's my older-by-ten-minutes twin brother, Rio, who's also our clan leader. He's sort of grumpy, but it's just a façade. Play your cards right, and you'll see how he's a big softie inside."

Rio grunted. "I heard that, Sol."

Solana shrugged. "I only speak the truth."

Axel's lips twitched, but Rio's face remained stony and unreadable. Although that was probably a requirement or something for a dragon clan leader, for all Jenny knew.

Wanting to make a good impression, Jenny smiled at both of the dragonmen as she exited the basket. After Axel kissed his mate and put an arm around her waist, hauling her to his side, his blue eyes met hers. "So this is the human Daniel rescued."

"Er, yes. I'm Jenny Hartmann."

Like usual, her nervousness made her do something stupid and she half-curtsied in her jeans.

Solana laughed. "Don't start that, Jenny, or my mate is going to expect all of us to start bowing to him. Which won't ever happen."

He grunted. "Maybe only you. I might be able to get some newcomers on board, though." He leaned down and whispered something into Solana's ear. Her mouth dropped open, but Solana quickly recovered and said, "But really, just act normally. It's not like clan leaders or head Protectors are royalty, or anything." She gestured toward Rio. "In the clan leader's case, they have to win a competition, prove their skills, and gain the clan's support."

Jenny knew that, of course. Since the clan leader trials often had all kinds of tasks and missions, large areas were sometimes closed off during the event. It'd happened on this mountain a number of years ago, she'd heard from her sister and her husband. "Er, yes. I know. It's just, well, reading or hearing about something is a whole lot different from experiencing it firsthand." She waved toward the basket. "Flying was a lot smoother than I'd imagined."

The clan leader finally spoke again. "Chris is one of the best flyers we have." He stared at Jenny with flashing dragon eyes, but she didn't even blink. He gave a small nod, as if she'd just passed a test, and Rio continued, "But there's a lot we should talk about, Jenny. Both about your stay here, and what Daniel shared with you."

"I know." She bit her bottom lip before replying, "But first, were there any updates while I was in the air?"

Rio shook his head. "Not much. Everyone reached the cabin, and they split into two groups—one for land and one for air. We might not hear anything else until it's all over."

A woman she hadn't noticed before, with curly black hair and dark skin, walked up to her. "It's frustrating, I know. My mate is one of the Protectors out there, too. But they all have each other's back— most of them have served together for years—and will do whatever it takes to bring everyone home in one piece." She smiled. "Oh, I didn't introduce myself. My name is Bree. Nice to meet you."

Blinking at how yet another dragon-shifter was so nice to her from the get go—despite the fact a lot of humans had made their lives hell over the years—she managed to reply, "Um, thanks. That helps a little, although I'm not sure I'll be completely sane again until Daniel returns. Oh, and I'm Jenny."

Bree gestured toward the opening in the rock walls surrounding the open area. "Come on, let's get you inside before you freeze to death. You can help me with getting warm drinks and meals ready for when they return."

She looked at Solana, who nodded. "Go with Bree. I'll find you soon, I promise."

Jenny waved goodbye and followed Bree. "Er, I should come clean—I'm not the best cook in the world."

The dragonwoman's pupils flashed before she grinned. "As long as it's not charcoal, they'll eat it. Humans have no idea how much a dragon-shifter can eat after prolonged periods of flying or maneuvers."

Feeling more at ease, she quipped, "More than human teenage boys?"

Bree shrugged. "I've never met one, but I somehow doubt it. One time, my mate ate three whole roasted chickens, four baked potatoes, a bowl of salad, and an entire cake in one sitting. How he didn't waddle afterward, I have no clue."

She laughed, liking Bree more and more. True, Solana had been nice, but Jenny didn't feel the need to impress as much; after all, Bree was just a normal clan member and not mated to the head of security.

They went inside a cute, small cabin with lots of big windows. Jenny did her best to help with making some sandwiches, and even started to feel more at home than she had in a long, long time when there was a pounding on the door.

Frowning, Bree went to answer it, and Jenny followed. When the door opened, Solana stood there. She stated, "You need to come quickly, Jenny. Daniel's been hurt, and it's serious."

All the calm, cozy feelings from earlier drained away. "He's hurt?"

"Yes. The human he took down had a small explosive in his backpack. While Daniel had knocked it away—which is why he's not dead already—it was still close enough to do a lot of damage." She gestured. "The doctors want you nearby. Sometimes a mate can help encourage someone to recover, to come back from the edge, when no one else can."

She wanted to say she wasn't Daniel's mate yet—didn't even know if they were actually true mates—but quickly pushed that thought aside. "I'll do whatever it takes to help Daniel."

Solana nodded. "Then grab your coat and come with me."

Jenny barely noted the walk to the small clinic building. No, the entire way her imagination kept coming up with the worst ideas, what could've gone wrong, and how her falling too fast for a guy was about to bite her in the ass yet again.

She wasn't quite ready to say she loved Daniel, but not having the chance to get to know him, feel his warm body wrapped around hers in bed again, or make him smile and laugh, made her gut churn.

Once inside the three-story building that Solana said was the clinic, a dragonman dressed in blue scrubs came up to them. He put out a hand, and Jenny shook on autopilot. He said, "I'm one of the nurses here, Matt. Come on, we'll go to a private waiting room. That way, as soon as the doctor says it's okay, you can visit Daniel."

Emotion choked her throat, but she managed to ask, "How is he?"

"I don't know all the specifics, but he's still alive. And if Dr. Baker has anything to say about it, he'll stay that way."

She tried to smile, but couldn't quite manage it.

As soon as they were inside a small room with a sofa, a plush chair, a small fridge, and even a sink,

Matt closed the door and said, "You'll have regular updates. Sit, try to drink something to keep up your strength, and I'll be back soon to check on you."

As the door clicked closed, Jenny paced the room. While she knew the nurse had to say those sorts of things, there was no way in hell she could just sit on the couch and sip a soda, or act casual.

Daniel had not only saved her from the cold and took her in, he'd ensured that his clan had taken her to safety. Not only that, he'd made his clan promise to look after her.

And he'd done all that after such a short acquaintance.

Add in how a simple caress or kiss on her neck made her melt, and Jenny had a hard time imagining a future without Daniel.

Oh, she wasn't quite ready to say it would all be perfect, and they'd live happily ever after. But she wanted to give them a chance and see what the future held.

Plus, she couldn't wait to hear his voice, feel his arms around her, and to have him make her feel beautiful and desired again.

All things she'd never really experienced with a man before.

As she paced, Jenny vowed to do whatever she could to help Daniel. And not just because she owed him, big time, for saving her life. No, because the world needed more people like him and it wasn't his time to go yet.

Chapter Thirteen

Hours later, Jenny sat on a couch, her head in her hands, and willed herself to take a power nap. It'd been eighteen hours since she'd arrived in this room, and no matter how much she didn't want to fall asleep, her body was starting to shut down on its own.

Five minutes of shut eye would be better than passing out and someone trying to wake her; she always was a heavy sleeper, no matter the situation.

As her mind buzzed with yet more possibilities of how Daniel had died already, the door opened. Raising her head, she spotted someone she hadn't seen before, a tall man wearing scrubs and his long, brown hair pulled back from his face into a man bun.

Standing, she blurted, "Any news?"

The dragonman—his green eyes had already flashed—answered, "Yes. However, before I can let you leave this room, I have to lay out all the facts. Because what we need to ask of you could change your entire future."

Her heart pounded. That sounded ominous. "W-what are you talking about?"

The man cleared his throat. "First, I'm Dr. Baker. As for Daniel, in the early hours after surgery, he was stable. But in the last few hours, his vital signs have slowly deteriorated. If we don't do something drastic, I'm afraid he'll crash and maybe die."

Her stomach dropped. She breathed, "No."

"However, you might be able to help."

She took a step toward the dragonman, wanting to shake him for withholding information for even a second longer than necessary. "How can I help him? Tell me. I'll do anything."

The dragonman frowned. "I can't just say yes without you knowing something first, so let me explain quickly: the best way to stabilize a dragon-shifter is to stir their inner dragon to life. If their dragon half fights to live, they usually pull through. And while friends or family are better than nothing, one person has the greatest chance of success in encouraging the dragon half—the patient's true mate."

And just like that, doom and gloom fell back over her. "I-I don't know if I'm his. So I might not help him after all."

Dr. Baker tilted his head. "Daniel informed Axel that you're probably his true mate. In retrospect, it was smart to give us that knowledge so we could use it." The doctor studied her a beat, his green eyes almost reaching inside her with their intensity before he added, "But if you kiss Daniel on the lips and he is your true mate, then his dragon will push his way to the forefront of Daniel's mind, determined to claim you."

She tried to process everything the doctor told her and struggled. "Wait, from what I know, a dragon will stop at nothing to claim his mate. Will he then just throw me down and start the frenzy, despite his health?"

Dr. Baker shook his head. "No, I won't allow that to happen. It's not shared publicly with many humans, but we have a drug that can rein in an inner beast for a short while."

A smidgen of hope returned. If the doctor could contain his dragon, she might be able to help Daniel after all.

But she doubted it was a long-term solution. Even she knew inner dragons were an integral part of a dragon-shifter. And before she committed to this plan, she needed to ask, "And what happens if I kiss him, stir his dragon, and then don't want to go through the frenzy?"

Jenny hated asking it, didn't even want to think it would come to that, and yet, she didn't want to force Daniel to take her as his mate without any say in the matter.

The doctor didn't miss a beat, as if expecting her question. "If a true mate rejects a dragon-shifter, then they have to remain isolated and mostly alone for at least a year until their need to claim fades. Otherwise, he'll search for you endlessly, until he finds you."

Just the thought of Daniel all but being imprisoned because she freaked out and ran made her stomach churn and twist.

The doctor leaned forward. "I hate to put this huge decision in front of you so quickly, but will you kiss Daniel and see if it stirs his inner dragon? All the while knowing you'll either have to commit to the mate-claim frenzy or flee somewhere distant until his dragon's need dies down?"

Her heart pounded harder, as she tried to take it all in.

Yes, she wanted Daniel to get better. And she wanted to help him.

But if, and it was still a big if, she was his true mate? Was Jenny prepared to commit herself to him, along with a baby, despite knowing him for such a short time?

Or the alternative was to flee everything she knew to hide from him?

Despite everything, she couldn't imagine running from Daniel. And while she'd been burned with a guy in the past, had fallen too quickly and made rash decisions, she sensed dragon-shifters were fundamentally different when it came to commitments as important as mates.

Needing confirmation, she asked, "Just tell me one more thing—what if we have the frenzy, I have his baby, and he regrets it? Because in a way, we're taking the choice away from him."

The dragon doctor shook his head. "No, we aren't. Daniel already told his friend he planned to mate you, no matter what it took."

She blinked. "He did?"

Dr. Baker nodded. "Yes. So it really comes down to you, Jenny. I know it's a lot to ask, and it will drastically change your future—you'll have to live with a dragon clan if you carry a half dragon baby—but you are our best hope for saving Daniel. And no matter what the future holds, we'll help you in any way that we can. You may not be officially part of our clan, but if Daniel was already determined to mate you, then we'll honor his intentions and protect you as if you really were his mate." He stepped closer. "So what do you say?"

She stared at the doctor, her mind whirring, and despite the million reasons why she should take more time, her gut screamed her answer. After all, Daniel had done more for her in a scant few days than her ex had done in years.

Daniel Torres was simply worth fighting for.

Taking a deep breath, Jenny nodded. "I'll do it."

Dr. Baker nodded. "Good. Then come with me."

"Already?"

"Yes, every minute we wait puts his life in greater danger."

Wow, this doctor really didn't pull his punches.

But Jenny had made her decision. She did them quickly, most of the time, and while they weren't always great—her ex-boyfriend being the prime example—she committed.

Daniel's room wasn't far away, and before she knew it, the doctor opened a room and gestured for her to follow.

Taking yet another deep breath to steel herself for what she might find, Jenny entered.

And barely suppressed a gasp.

Daniel lay in a hospital bed, his face bruised, cut, and even burned in a few places. He was hooked up to all types of machines, beeping and doing who knew what. And not only was his skin a sickly pale color, but was also still. So unnaturally still.

But then her gaze fixated on the rise and fall of his

chest, and it gave her the strength to approach him. As long as he breathed, there was still a chance to save him.

Jenny stopped next to the bed. Without taking her gaze from Daniel's battered face, she asked the doctor, "Can I take his hand first?"

"Yes, just be gentle."

Jenny wrapped her fingers around his. Even if his skin was cooler than before, the contact sent a rush of rightness, security, and all-around contentment through her.

She wanted a chance with this dragonman. Desperately.

Dr. Baker stood across from her, on the opposite side of the bed. "Anytime you're ready. Just nod at me before you kiss him, so I can be prepared."

He'd already donned some clean gloves and opened a drawer near the bed. Not wanting to look at what lay inside—there was a reason she'd gone to school to be a teacher and not a nurse or doctor—she lightly brushed the uninjured skin at Daniel's temple and whispered, "Thank you for saving me. Now it's my turn to do the same."

After nodding at Dr. Baker, Jenny lowered her head and gently pressed her lips to Daniel's.

Even if it was fairly chaste, and not more than a brush of skin, the contact made her entire body wake up, ready for more.

Oh yes, this was the man for her. No one else had this effect on her.

After lingering a few seconds, she pulled back and frowned. Daniel didn't respond, didn't move, nothing.

Did that mean she wasn't his true mate, after all?

And why did that fact make her chest tighten and eyes prickle with tears?

Daniel's eyes flew open, his pupils flashing, and his voice was deeper than normal. "You're mine, human. Mine. And I need to claim you to keep the other males away."

She blinked. Before she could ask, Dr. Baker said, "Yes, you're his true mate. Now, step back so I can help him."

Jenny tried to walk backwards, but Daniel's grip on her hand tightened, keeping her in place. That deeper voice—was it his dragon?—growled, "Don't go. I need my mate. Now."

She shook her head. "Later. Right now, you're hurt and need to rest."

Daniel growled. "I need to claim my mate to keep the other males away."

Dr. Baker was preparing a syringe, and Jenny kept talking to distract Daniel. "I don't want any other males, Daniel. Just you."

He growled. "Words aren't enough. I need to fuck you, over and over again, until you carry our child."

Well, his dragon was most definitely blunt.

Before Jenny could think of how to answer that, Dr. Baker pulled the empty syringe from Daniel's arm. Within seconds, Daniel's voice was groggy as his eyelids struggled to stay open. "What did you do to…"

His body went slack, and he fell unconscious. Jenny waited, watching his chest. When he continued to breathe in a steady rhythm, she let out a sigh of relief. "Will he be okay now and pull through?"

"Most likely." She must've let fear show on her face because the dragon doctor gentled his tone. "I don't lie to my patients, Jenny. There's always a chance things could go wrong. However, I put his recovery at about a 95 percent chance of success, thanks to you."

As she stared back at Daniel's face, she brushed some hair off his forehead. She really, really hated that remaining five percent.

The doctor's voice garnered her attention again. "What I need you to do is go stay with Bree, get some rest, and come back tomorrow."

Never taking her gaze from Daniel's slack face, she shook her head. "I can't leave him. What if you need me again?"

"His dragon will be silent for a few days. I also gave him something that will make him sleep so his body can heal. He won't wake up before tomorrow morning."

"But…"

"Jenny." And Dr. Baker's firm tone, she met his gaze again. "If Daniel learns we didn't take care of you—ensure you're fed, rested, and protected—he'll give us hell when he wakes up. And personally, I don't need a grumpy, growly dragonman following me around, being a pain in my ass. So go to Bree's place, eat and sleep, and then come back refreshed."

She bit her lip, still undecided. It felt wrong to leave him like this.

The doctor lowered his head until she noticed and met his gaze. He said, "Here's something you may not know: A dragon-shifter loves to see their mate—or future mate—happy, more than anything. When he sees you're well when he wakes up, it'll make him happy and maybe even help him heal faster."

She saw through the guilt-tripping, but couldn't

blame the doctor. Dealing with sick and injured dragon-shifters on a regular basis couldn't be easy. Even if her experience was limited, she was starting to understand more and more how the dragons thought and acted.

In other words, Daniel would worry if she came back looking like the undead, with giant dark circles under her eyes, and her skin pale from low blood sugar. "Fine, I'll try my best, although I can't stop myself from worrying. I'll come back as early as possible tomorrow, and I'll stay until you kick me out again."

Dr. Baker smiled. "I think you're going to fit in here fine, Jenny."

That was probably a compliment, but she was too tired to analyze it further. "I hope so." She looked back at Daniel. "Because Daniel belongs here, and I want to be near him."

To his credit, the doctor didn't snort. Because even to her own ears, it sounded a little needy and cheesy.

But she didn't care. Jenny was his true mate, after all. Fate thought she would be his best chance at happiness.

She only hoped it worked out that way.

Chapter Fourteen

P ain radiated through Daniel's entire body, although it seemed far away, dull, almost as if it belonged to someone else.

That was his first thought. His second was how quiet and empty his mind felt, as if his dragon had disappeared. Since he'd first talked with his inner dragon over twenty years ago, it was incredibly strange and lonely.

Did that mean he was dead? Everything was dark, after all.

Although something prodded him to try opening his eyes. It took a lot of concentration, and way more fucking effort than it should, but finally his eyelids opened and a dim light filled his vision.

After blinking a few seconds, the room came into focus. Judging from the machines, beige walls, and the door with the rectangular window in the upper half, he was inside the clan's clinic.

Everything rushed back to him—the first explosion, getting Jenny to safety, exploring the forest, and finally tackling the human male as another explosion went off.

He tried reaching into his mind for his dragon, but nothing. No presence, no mental image, no growling or complaining about something.

Before he could start to panic—it was rare, but possible for a dragon-shifter to lose their inner dragon —a female voice filled his ears. "Daniel! You're awake!"

Jenny was at his side, gripping his hand, with tears in her eyes. Her presence helped ease some of his anxiety.

Because she was safe.

He croaked, "Jenny."

She nodded. "Yes, it's me. Thank goodness you finally woke up. Everyone was getting worried."

He didn't like how bloodshot her eyes were, or how pale her skin was. And yet, instead of asking when she last ate or slept, he blurted, "How long was I out?"

"Four days, but it seemed like years." She gently raised his hand and kissed the back. Her lips brushing his skin calmed him. She continued, "And Dr. Baker said to tell you that your dragon should be back when you're ready. He just had to silence him for a little while after we, er, kissed."

He'd kissed her? And he didn't fucking remember it?

He must've growled out loud because Jenny laughed. "Yes, you were unconscious at the time— definitely a Sleeping Beauty vibe—and then you were given meds to sleep. So that's why you probably don't remember it. Although it wasn't some passionate, devouring kiss, so you didn't miss much."

He growled again. "I still wish I fucking remember it."

She smiled as she brushed the hair from his forehead, and Daniel leaned into her touch. Her voice was softer as she said, "I know. But it was either kiss you while you were unconscious and stir your dragon, or probably watch you die. And I couldn't do that, Daniel."

Her voice cracked, and he reached for her hand. It felt like lifting fifty pounds, but as soon as he wrapped his fingers around hers and she squeezed, he saw Jenny relax a bit.

Good. Because even still somewhat sleepy, he'd put together why the doctor had drugged him unconscious. "So you are my true mate, like my dragon thought."

She dropped her gaze. "Yes."

He didn't like how she fell silent. Even though it hurt his heart to ask it, he did. "Did you not want to be?"

Her eyes met his again and widened. "Oh, no, I did want to be your true mate. Well, I didn't really think I wanted it as much as I did once it happened. But it's kind of strange to know that once you're better, we'll be secluded somewhere, having sex over and over again, until I'm pregnant. Kind of like a fast-forward button to life, or something. Although at this rate, we'll probably have to hit rewind a few times before we finally reach the end."

He couldn't help but smile at her rambling.

Despite everything, she was still the Jenny he'd known before shit had hit the fan, and that reassured him.

Especially since she said she wanted to be his mate. His. This female would be his to win, to cherish, and make happy.

Now, if he could only heal faster and get his ass out of this bed, he could start working on it all. "We can take some time until you're more comfortable with the idea of a mate-claim frenzy." He squeezed her fingers and lowered his voice. "But I won't lie—I've wanted you naked and at my mercy since the beginning."

She raised an eyebrow. "You saw me sitting on my ass on the icy road, shouting at nothing, and thought, 'Oh, yeah, baby. I want her in my bed.'"

He chuckled. "Okay, maybe not that exact moment, but soon after. But definitely as I carried your warm, lush body in my arms."

Even to his own ears, his voice had turned husky. Jenny's cheeks flushed. "Calm down, dragonman. We can't even kiss again until the doctor clears you, let alone go at it like rabbits."

His lips twitched. "If you call it 'going at it like rabbits,' then you've clearly never had good sex."

"Maybe not." She cleared her throat. "But given our, er, earlier playtime, we should be fine in that department." He growled, and she added, "Okay, more than fine. Wonderful. Earth-shattering. Supercalifragilisticexpialidocious, even."

He laughed. "Try calling that out when you come, my human. I dare you."

She shook her head. "If I can, then it means you're not trying hard enough."

He snorted. "Fair point."

As they grinned at one another, Daniel temporarily forgot all about his injuries, or his road to recovery, or any remaining enemies out there who might attack. No, right here, right now, he was exactly where he should be—with his true mate, the human he loved.

Because, yes, he couldn't imagine living without her silliness, or chattiness, or willingness to stand up to him.

She was his perfect fit, and together, he knew they could face anything.

Not that he'd tell her that just yet. No, she'd just had a lot of shit thrown at her, out of nowhere, and needed time to process it all.

He'd tell her his feelings when the time was right. For now, he merely gripped her hand tighter in his and said, "At least give me a quick kiss, one I can actually remember this time."

She lifted his hand and kissed it again. "And before you growl, or grunt, or whatever, the doctor said not to risk kissing your mouth until you're well, since it could stir your dragon."

Who'd be hell-bent on fucking Jenny until she was pregnant.

With a sigh, he asked, "Where's Kyle?" At her blank look, he clarified, "Dr. Baker?"

"Oh, I already pushed the call button, so he should be here any moment."

And before he could lift her hand to his mouth and kiss it, Kyle strode in, confident as ever.

While Daniel knew any dragon-shifter doctor had to be somewhat apart from the clan in order to treat them effectively, he still missed the male he'd grown up with—the carefree, fun-loving guy who took risks.

He still took risks, but now as a profession and never in his personal life.

Maybe he needed to find a female of his own to shake things up.

Kyle stopped at the side of his bed. "Since you've woken up, I've upped your recovery chances to 99 percent."

He groaned. "Not the percentages again."

The doctor smirked. "Yes, I still use them. That hasn't changed in the weeks since I last saw you. Now, I need to ask some questions and check a few things." Kyle looked at Jenny. "Maybe you can grab a coffee or a snack while I do it?"

Jenny shook her head. "I'm staying."

Even though his human stood at least eight inches shorter than the doctor, she kept her head high and didn't back down.

Yes, more and more, he thought she'd do well with his clan.

Kyle cleared his throat. "Fine. Just move and get out of the way when I tell you to, okay? The sooner I finish this, the sooner I can come up with a recovery plan and give you two some time alone." He gave Daniel a stern, I'm-the-doctor-so-heed-me look. "But absolutely no sex, not even oral or a hand job. You need to keep your heart rate and blood pressure down for the next few days."

Jenny blinked, probably not used to doctors referencing hand jobs during a consultation. But with dragon-shifters, sex was important, not embarrassing, and discussed freely.

Daniel grunted. "Fine. Although you'd better do your damnedest to get me better as soon as possible. I have a mate to claim."

Kyle rolled his eyes. "Yes, yes, I've heard it all before. Now, let's start with the questions…"

And as the doctor asked boring things, like if he knew his name or what day it'd been the last time he'd been awake, Daniel kept sneaking glances at Jenny. Every time she smiled at him, his annoyance slipped away and the world turned brighter again.

Although when Kyle said it'd be nearly two weeks before he could finally claim Jenny, he knew it was going to be the longest two weeks of his life.

He'd just have to distract himself by getting to know his mate, find out what he could do to take care of her, help her, and be her partner in all things.

Because being a dragon's true mate wasn't just about a mate-claim frenzy and the amazing sex. No, Daniel would ensure Jenny never wanted to leave him, no matter how rough things might get in the future.

And given their whirlwind story so far, it probably wouldn't be easy. And yet, Daniel was stubborn and was up to the task. Jenny was worth it, and that's all that mattered.

Chapter Fifteen

Over the next two weeks, Jenny spent as much time as possible with Daniel. She'd learned how competitive he was with card or board games—but she hadn't backed down, ever, since she liked to win too—and had even met his mother for the first time.

Rosa Maria Torres was quieter than Jenny—which wasn't hard to do—but kind with a backbone of steel. Seeing her get Daniel to rest when he didn't want to had been funny to watch.

Rosa Maria had also been welcoming, not batting an eyelash at her son's true mate being human.

It'd been so long since Jenny's mother had been alive that she'd almost started crying when Rosa Maria had said she looked forward to having her as a daughter-in-law and hugged her. Thankfully, she'd held it together until she was alone with Daniel, and then she'd spilled everything about how she still missed her mom, hadn't really known her dad since he'd died young, and how her sister and her had become a united front, ready to face the world.

Unfortunately, her sister couldn't come to Clan MirrorPeak until after Jenny officially mated Daniel, which would happen as soon as the frenzy was over. She still talked to her sister daily, and had been given one tip after another about how to be married—or mated, the same thing Jessica said—and not kill each other over one misplaced dirty dish.

Apparently, that had been a near thing once with her sister and her husband.

But while Daniel was sometimes grumpy, or less talkative than she'd like, she was more than aware she had her difficulties, too. Regardless, when they were alone, the world just seemed more right, more at peace, more perfect.

Although, as she paced the living room of what was Daniel's cabin, she did her best not to chew her lower lip and make it bleed. Bree sighed. "Stop worrying. Mate-claim frenzies are like nothing else. Trust me, you'll never have so many orgasms in a row in your life again, and you'll also learn to love how the dragon's sexual playtime is different from the human's."

It was still weird to think of two personalities existing in one mind, but Jenny always tried her best to understand. "I'm not worried about that. Just kissing Daniel makes me hot and ready to jump him. But I still worry everything is moving so fast. Clan MirrorPeak hasn't had a human living here in a long, long time. And I haven't had the time to win everyone over, or at least figure out who to watch out for."

Bree shook her head. "Leave that to us, at least for

now. We won't let anything happen to you, nor will Daniel, once he's back to full-fighting strength."

She nodded. "I know that rationally, but I still worry. My life has been a bit of a disaster for the last four years or so. I have a hard time accepting that things are so amazing and will stay that way."

The dragonwoman smiled. "You'll get there, eventually. Sometimes true mates find out with a mistaken kiss, and sex and pregnancy come before any sort of feelings. While that wasn't my story, I've heard about some of the Tahoe Dragon Mate lottery humans in the past who've struggled. Not all, but some."

"Are they all still together?"

"Mostly. But don't constantly imagine everything will go wrong, or you'll doom yourself before you've even tried. And I know some of your doubts—or have guessed them, at any rate—and you have nothing to worry about. Your ex was a dick, selfish, and not worthy of someone like you." She winked. "Dragon-shifters are better, anyway."

She laughed at the dragonwoman's playful tone. "Sometimes. Humans have their uses, too. Like how we don't stand there for minutes on end, talking with a dragon inside our head, and then make everyone else shuffle their feet, waiting for them to finish."

Bree shrugged. "It's only because you didn't grow up that way. To a human, though, yes, it can be a little strange or awkward. But when you mate a dragon-shifter, you get both halves." She studied Jenny a beat before adding, "Even though you haven't had much time getting to know Daniel's dragon, are you willing to accept him? He'll become a lot more vocal in decision making, going forward."

She'd thought long and hard about this, but she trusted Daniel, so she'd trust his dragon, too. "I know. If nothing else, the mate-claim frenzy will give me a crash course to better knowing his dragon."

The doorbell sounded and Jenny stopped pacing, rubbing her hands up and down her skirt—she'd chosen a simple dress she wasn't attached to, per Bree's instructions, since it would probably be shredded— and did her best to calm her racing heart. "This is it."

The dragonwoman placed a hand on her shoulder and squeezed. "You've got this. Besides, once you have all that muscled dragonman to yourself, you'll probably only be able to drool and think of little else but getting his cock into your pussy."

Her cheeks heated. "Bree!"

She laughed. "Hey, teasing is part of the fun." She sobered. "I'll leave out the back door. Go to him and have fun, Jenny. By the end, you'll truly be bound to him—as well as to MirrorPeak—forever through your child."

Not wanting to think of her unknown baby as she slept with Daniel for the first time—it wasn't exactly sexy to think of vomit and constantly filled diapers— she strode toward the door and willed her mind blank.

Although once she opened the door to Daniel standing in jeans and a rather tight T-shirt, her mouth dropped open a little.

At least she hadn't drooled. Yet.

He smirked. "You act as if you haven't seen me out of the clinic before."

His words snapped her back to the present. "Well, it wasn't for long, you know. I was starting to think hospital gowns, complete with your ass hanging out, were the norm. Although come to think of it, I'm going to miss peeks of that ass."

He laughed, strode inside, shut the door, and turned her around until her back gently met the wood. He lowered his face, and his pupils flashed. She squeaked, "How is your dragon not in control?"

Nuzzling her cheek, he murmured, "Oh, he keeps going on about fucking you, yes. But I made a bargain with him to claim you for the first time."

He kissed her jaw, her cheek, her nose, and then stopped an inch from her lips. As his hot breath caressed her skin, she had to concentrate to ask, "What bargain?"

Daniel stroked her cheek with his fingers, and she sighed happily. He murmured, "Oh, that he can take you twice in a row after the first time. But after that, we take turns."

Maybe she should be a little worried about having sex twice in a row with a dragon hell-bent on impregnating her—it'd be rougher and quicker, according to Bree—and yet all she could think about was kissing Daniel and finally tasting him.

She leaned forward, but he retreated an inch. He smiled as he said, "You kissed me first to wake my dragon, remember? This time, I'm going to be the one kissing you. That way, we've both made our first claims."

Dragon-shifters really took their claiming stuff seriously.

But Daniel pressed his lips to hers, and all reason fled her mind.

He was slow and gentle at first, merely teasing her lips. But then his tongue swiped across her mouth, and she opened and he took his first possessive lick.

Groaning, she leaned against his hard body, grabbing his shirt to keep him close, and met him stroke for stroke, lick for lick, and all around lost herself in the taste, and heat, and possessiveness of her dragonman.

Jenny had never thought herself one to want a demanding man, but with Daniel, oh, it was so, so good.

He pulled her away from the door and gripped her ass with his hands, rocking her against him. She moaned as her clit rubbed against his jean-clad cock. "I've been dreaming of this."

After another quick, deep kiss, he replied, "Me too. Every second of every damned day."

Before she could even blink at that, he lifted, and she wrapped her legs around his waist. Maybe with another man, she'd protest about being too heavy. But with Daniel, she always felt safe, perfect, and had zero worries that he'd drop her.

She didn't know how long they kissed and clung to each other before Daniel pulled away and growled, "I need to get you into a bed. Now."

"Then do it."

He walked, supporting her against him, into the bedroom. She'd never been in here before since she'd stayed with Bree over the last two weeks. However, she didn't even look at the furniture or any of the decorations because Daniel had her on his bed, ripped her dress away, and towered over her before she could blink.

He ran a hand over her belly, up, up, until he could cup her breast. Lowering his head, he took her nipple into his mouth and suckled. Hard.

She arched her back and spread her legs, wanting more than his mouth on her breast. No, she wanted to finally feel his cock inside her, claiming her, fulfilling all those dreams and fantasies she'd had of this moment.

A hand brushed her clit, and she jumped. Daniel slowly stroked over her pussy, up, and then back down to tease her opening, never touching where she throbbed most for his touch. "Stop teasing me. I've waited too long for this."

He released her nipple and smiled. "You sound just like a dragon-shifter." She narrowed her eyes, and he laughed. "Fine, I've wanted to fuck you hard, and then take you slow and gentle, and then hard again." He brushed his lips against hers in a whisper of a kiss. "Time to claim my mate for real."

Daniel stepped back, and she reached for him. He shook his head. "I need to undress, Jenny."

He quickly shed his clothes—damn, he was toned everywhere, although her gaze lingered on his hard, heavy cock as it bobbed—and then he crawled over, until he was above her on his hands and knees. "Ready?"

She gripped his fine, taut ass cheeks and squeezed. "More than ready."

With a growl, he lowered his body until he lay on her, but not with his full weight; he supported himself on his elbows and arms.

Although she could feel his very hard, very thick cock pressing against her belly, and she squirmed, wetness rushing between her thighs.

He kissed her, taking his time to lap, and suckle her tongue, and all around explored her mouth until he lifted his head for air. As they both breathed heavily, he murmured, "I need to claim you soon, or my dragon's going to break free. But just know that later, much later, I'll take you slowly, tease you with my tongue until you beg to come, and then finally give it to you." He caressed her cheek, his touch so gentle yet possessive at the same time. "And you'll tell me all your fantasies and desires so I can fulfill them, Jenny. But until the frenzy is complete, it's going to be a lot of hot, quick, and rather desperate sex."

She looped her arms around his neck. "Sounds perfect."

With a growl, he kissed her again as he placed his cock at her entrance. She was so wet, and swollen, and her clit ached more than it ever had before.

She wanted this dragonman, desperately, and she was finally, finally, about to have him.

He pushed slowly inside, and she gasped. He was so damned thick. "Daniel."

"Shh, love. I'll take it slow at first."

Jenny wasn't a virgin, but it'd been nearly a year since she'd last had sex, and damn, she wasn't sure Daniel would fit.

But he kissed her, and tweaked her nipple, and lightly brushed her clit with firm, slow strokes, and soon her legs melted open more and more. And as Daniel finally slipped inside to the hilt with a growl, she purred.

He nipped her bottom lip. "You're so fucking tight, and hot, and perfect, love. Better than any dream or fantasy."

She had zero time to doubt his words because Daniel moved his hips, slowly at first, and Jenny couldn't do anything but moan, or cry out, or dig her nails into Daniel's back.

He wasn't slow, or teasing, or any of the things he'd promised to do later. No, he soon thrust harder and harder, the bed shaking, and she couldn't help but blurt, "Harder, Daniel. Don't stop."

And unlike her human lovers, he didn't. No, he kissed her as he thrust harder. Not like a piston, but out, and then in deliberately. The friction was delicious, especially as his lower pelvis hit her clit each time.

She'd never come from a man merely thrusting before, but Daniel was careful to hit her clit, enough that she soon shouted his name as she came, wave after wave of pleasure coursing through her body.

He soon stilled. And as she'd been told, his semen sent her spiraling into another orgasm, confirming she was his true mate.

She didn't know how long it went on, but eventually her pussy stilled and Daniel lifted his head. The look of awe and reverence in his gaze shot straight to her heart. He murmured, "It's never been like that before."

And she'd wanted to say it would only be that way with her because he was hers as much as she was his.

However, Daniel's pupils turned to slits and stayed that way. "My turn."

His dragon was now in charge.

DANIEL HAD WANTED to stay lying on top of Jenny forever, her soft body cushioning his hard one, his cock nestled deep in her perfect pussy.

But he'd barely been able to muster the strength to murmur a few words before his dragon rushed to the front of his mind and said, *It's my turn. She's our mate, ours. And she needs to carry our child, to let all the other males know she belongs to us, and only us.*

Since arguing with his beast in the midst of a mate-claim frenzy was a waste of time, Daniel merely said, *Just remember—twice and then I get her again. I need to make sure she has food and enough rest to keep going.*

I know. I'd never hurt our mate.

And then his dragon shoved Daniel to the back of their mind and all he could do was watch as his dragon took control of their body.

His dragon growled, "My turn."

Jenny nodded. "I know. So claim me already."

Fuck, she was challenging his dragon. And while his beast loved it and nearly purred at her words, he only hoped his beast wouldn't be too rough this early. *Remember, she's never been with a dragon-shifter before.*

His beast ignored him, pulled out, and then rose to their knees. He flipped Jenny on her belly, raised her hips, and lightly smacked her ass.

And his mate raised her butt in the air more, spreading her legs, showcasing her cunt to them.

Where she already glistened.

At the sight, his dragon growled, positioned their cock at her pussy, and thrust. "My human, always mine. No other male will touch you. Ever."

His dragon pulled out and thrust. He held her hips in place, moving quickly, caring about nothing but their orgasm so they could fill Jenny with more of their seed.

Although she moaned and obviously liked his dragon's rough fucking, Daniel wanted her to come before they did. *Touch her clit.*

No, it's my turn. I just want to fuck her, over and over again, until she carries our scent and child.

Dragon, make her come. We need to take care of her, remember? All mates do.

As his beast continued to piston his hips, Daniel tried to think of another way to convince his dragon to see to their mate's pleasure. It wouldn't be easy, given how the dragon half was more instinctual. And right now, his beast only cared about breeding.

However, to his surprise, his dragon moved a hand around to Jenny's front, over her soft belly, and then down until he could press against her clit.

Jenny cried out, arched her back, and she gripped and released their cock, repeatedly, even more intensely than before.

Maybe she enjoyed it a little rough.

Daniel itched to please his mate, to find out more about what she wanted, and fulfill her every fantasy. However, his dragon stilled, and they orgasmed, their cock shooting jet after jet of cum into their mate, making yet another claim, and soothing both man and beast.

Because, yes, even Daniel wanted her to carry his scent—which would happen once she was pregnant—to let the world know she was his.

Once his dragon finished, he pulled out, flipped

Jenny onto her back again, and stroked their already hardening cock. His beast said, "Again."

Even though Jenny breathed heavily, and her face was extremely flushed, she didn't hesitate to spread her legs. When she moved a hand to her clit and lightly stroked, both man and beast groaned.

She was getting more confident. Fuck, when he had a turn again, it was going to be fun.

His dragon didn't waste time claiming her again, and making them both orgasm within minutes.

Under normal circumstances, Daniel would scold his dragon. But for now, that meant it was his turn to be in charge and look after his mate.

Once his dragon finished coming, he didn't fight Daniel as he pushed to the front of their mind. As soon as his beast was curled up, probably to take a quick nap until his next turn, Daniel lay next to Jenny, pulled her close, and kissed her damp forehead. "So what's the verdict when it comes to sleeping with a dragonman?"

She smiled as she played with the light smattering of hair on his chest. "So you're back in charge then?"

He gripped her ass and gave a possessive squeeze. "Yes. So? What do you think?"

Jenny yawned—confirming what he'd thought, that she needed a break—and answered, "I can honestly say it's the best sex of my life. And not just because your orgasm triggers my own too."

He placed a finger under her chin and tilted her face to meet his gaze. At the contentment and happiness he saw, both man and beast hummed. "It's going to be like this for days and days. So I want you to promise to tell me if you need a break, or food, or anything else. Yes, my dragon will be horny as fuck until you're pregnant, but he would also never willingly cause you pain."

She smiled at him, making his heart lighten. He would never tire of that smile. "I will. I'm definitely going to need a Power Nap soon, though. Even if your dragon is rather quick, all those orgasms make a lady sleepy." She yawned again and added, "I know some women get super energized, but I think that's only because they've never been with a dragon-shifter before."

He stroked her hip, up to her ribcage, and back down again. He'd probably never tire of the urge to touch his mate. "Then a nap you shall have." He kissed her lips gently. "And when you're rested, it's my turn again, love. I may have to test how long my dragon will let me tease you before finally letting you come."

She snuggled against him. "Maybe we could make a game of it. I'm going to have to test your dragon's limits, after all."

His beast said sleepily, *I'll always win.*

Keep thinking that, dragon. Keep thinking that.

He said to Jenny, "He looks forward to it." He noticed her drooping eyelids, and he tugged a blanket over them. "Sleep, love. And if you want to eat when you wake up, we'll do that. No matter what, taking care of my mate will always be the most important thing."

Well, it would tie with protecting his future children. However, he only had Jenny in this moment, and he would do anything for her.

She murmured, "I don't know how, but I think I love you already, Daniel Torres."

Her words warmed his heart, and he was about to ask her to repeat them—just to make sure—but when he looked at his mate, she was fast asleep.

So he merely held her close, reveled in her heat and scent, and fell asleep soon after, dreaming of the future he wanted with his true mate.

Chapter Sixteen

J enny had lost count of the days of the frenzy after the first few. It basically became a blur of sex, food, sleep, and cleaning up.

Her dragonman's dragon half was a lusty one, and she didn't mind too much. A frenzy was a special thing, only happened once between two people, and Daniel had assured her his dragon would become almost boring once it was all over.

Although she highly doubted a dragon could ever be boring. Because, hello, he was a dragon.

Still, as she snuggled against the now familiar muscled form of Daniel, she bordered between sleep and alertness, trying to decide if she should just let her mind drift from topic to topic or if she should actually open her eyes and gear up for another round.

A hand rubbed her lower back, and she sighed. Daniel knew she was awake; dragon-shifters and their supernatural senses could be irritating sometimes. "I want to sleep some more."

His hand continued making circles, slowly, as if

trying to soothe her. She waited for him to move south, to squeeze her butt, or even tease her core.

However, his touch merely remained comforting. His deep voice rumbled beneath her ear on his chest. "If you're trying to feign sleep to avoid more sex, you don't have to, love. It's done."

She sucked in a breath. "What?"

"Look at me, Jenny."

After opening her eyes, she found Daniel's gaze. She found pride, tenderness, and something she wanted to say was love—but didn't think it could be—shining there.

Despite her exhaustion, she'd learned during their frenzy that she truly loved him, which was probably why she wished he felt the same.

He finally spoke again. "You carry my scent, Jenny, which means you carry my child."

He placed his other hand over her lower belly and tears suddenly sprang to her eyes. Not out of dread or sadness, or any sort of negative emotion. No, she rather liked the fact that a little of her and a little of Daniel was growing inside her.

At her dragonman's frown, she scooted up a little so she could kiss him. She took her time, teasing his lips, lightly darting her tongue inside his mouth and out again, merely tasting him because she wanted to.

Eventually, she pulled away and placed a hand on his cheek. As she stroked the light stubble there, she said, "I can't wait for that next step in the book of our lives, Daniel. Although I have so much to learn and prepare for, now that the frenzy is over. I'm not going to allow our child to try and pull one over on me because I'm human."

He grinned. "Oh, I'll help you, love. And if they try it, they'll learn soon not to." He nuzzled her cheek. "There's always community service around the clan they can do. Not to mention their mother will be pioneering new courses about humans for dragon-shifters, and vice versa. She might need help around the house to keep up with demand."

She laughed. "I haven't even written a word, let alone made an outline. It's going to take months, if not years, to do what I have planned."

"Which is perfect because babies can't exactly try to outsmart their parents with debate skills. That's going to take a few years of practice, at least."

He winked, and Jenny giggled at the image of a baby trying to win an argument with coos and gurgles. "You say that, but I remember when my nephews were little. And you'd be surprised what a wide-eyed look or smile will make you do, long before they can speak."

He grunted. "I'll be able to resist."

She rolled her eyes. "We'll see. There's a softy behind all that muscle. Our baby will probably wrap you around their fingers in the first week, if not the first day."

He kissed her nose. "We have some time before we have to worry about any of that. I fully expect to spoil my mate up until you go into labor, love. You're mine to protect, cherish, and love."

She almost bit her lip at his last word and debated telling him about her feelings.

In her experience, she'd always fallen first and had spooked her ex.

But then she remembered how Daniel was

different, how he'd always taken care of her, looked after her, and never had tried to make her feel bad about herself.

Well, shit-talking during a game didn't count, of course. They both egged each other then.

Just remembering the last game they'd played before the frenzy—a rather intense bout of Uno—made her smile.

Daniel kissed the corner of her mouth. "Tell me that smile is somehow related to me."

She laughed. "Now I'm tempted to say the opposite." He lightly smacked her ass, and she added, "Okay, okay, yes, it was. I recalled our last game of Uno, and you have to admit it was pretty intense, yet funny."

He chuckled. "I think you called me a devious asshole for making you pick up a bunch of cards."

She lightly poked his chest. "Considering you tried to hide a few under the blanket, you were a devious asshole."

As they stared at one another, smiling, Jenny decided to stop being afraid. "I love you, Daniel Torres. So much so, it hurts sometimes."

His pupils flashed a few times before he kissed her lips. "I love you too, Jenny Hartmann. Just being with you brightens my world, makes me want to try to be better, and do whatever I can to make you smile. You're my other half, love. And I can't wait to mate you."

Even as her heart brimmed with happiness, she couldn't resist teasing, "You haven't officially asked me anything yet."

With a growl, he rolled her onto her back, pinned

her arms above her head, and nipped her jaw. "Minx."

She wiggled and tried not to laugh. "Well, it's true. It's probably my only time ever being asked to mate or marry someone, and I want a good memory."

He growled. "It *will* be the only time."

She smiled at his grumpy tone. "Still waiting."

He kissed her, hard and possessive, exploring every inch of her mouth, making her breathless with each passing second. Once he broke the kiss, he rolled out of bed, went to one knee on the floor, and took one of her hands. "I think this is how humans do it, at least according to the movies."

Even though she would've mated Daniel if all he'd done was grunt out a few words to propose, the sight of him on a knee before her brought tears to her eyes. "Yes. Although I think we'll leave out the part about us being naked in the story."

His gaze raked over her breasts, open to the air after the blanket had fallen down. "I think you should always be naked when we're alone."

She shook her head. "I know that look. Now, hurry up and ask me so you, me, and your dragon can celebrate in this bed."

Daniel kissed the back of her hand and said firmly, "I had no idea that when I found you shouting in the middle of that icy road, sitting next to a car named Ol' Bess, that I'd found my future. While I knew from the second I had you in my arms that I desired you, it was only as I got to know you that I knew fate had picked the right female for me. You bring out my fun side, aren't afraid to tease me and face my growls, and you even accept my dragon half's lusty habits. You're everything I ever wanted, and we've barely begun our journey together. By the end, I'll have a book of reasons about why I love you. So, Jenny Hartmann, will you be my mate?"

She sniffled, trying not to cry. "That was beautiful, Daniel." He winked at her and she laughed, instantly knowing he was trying to lighten the mood again. "Yes, I'll mate you. Despite your grumpiness, or overprotectiveness, or even dissing my car Ol' Bess—may she rest in peace—you're still kind, understanding, playful, and the calm in the storm I need sometimes. I never would've thought that a dragon-shifter would be my perfect mate or husband, and yet I can't imagine growing old with anyone else. I love you, Daniel Torres. Will you be my mate?"

He grinned. "I didn't expect to be asked. Maybe you should get down on one knee." She narrowed her eyes, and he laughed. "Of course I'll be your mate." He stood, lay next to her, and murmured, "Especially since you didn't make me promise not to cheat at cards in the future."

She chuckled, and he kissed her. Before long, he was inside her, making love to her slowly, gently, as if wanting to prolong this memory forever.

And as they fell asleep murmuring, "I love you," to each other, Jenny knew she'd found the happy ending she'd never known she wanted.

Epilogue

Four Years Later

Jenny paced the living room, knowing she had a million things to do, but couldn't concentrate on any of them.

After all, she should receive the final copies of her first dragon-shifter textbook series for middle schoolers today.

She'd wanted to do the younger grades first, but Daniel and her sister had convinced her that the lessons in middle school were the most intense, longest, and probably made the biggest impression. So she'd started there.

And even with two kids under the age of four, she'd managed to do it—write a three-book series filled with the truth about dragon-shifters. No more conspiracy theories, or rumors, or pseudo bedtime stories meant to scare humans.

Her sister Jessica swayed in place with Jenny's youngest child—a daughter named Sofia—in her arms. Since the baby had only just fallen asleep, Jessica kept her voice low. "You know every word in those books five times over. Hell, I know them by now. And you did an amazing job, Jenny. So why are you this nervous?"

She shrugged. "They still could've edited it, taken things out, or anything else."

Jessica raised her brows. "Not with the contract my husband ironed out for you."

She tapped a hand against her thigh. "But—"

"No, just stop, Jenny. They'll be amazing, and pretty, and will truly help bridge the divide between my kids and yours, and for families all across the US who are a mixture of human and dragon-shifter. Not only that, but they'll help all humans and dragon-shifters over time."

"I hope so."

The front door opened and Daniel strode in, a box under one arm and their three-year-old son held in the other. Their son, Camden, held out his arms. "Mommy."

Daniel almost sighed, like always. Camden was most definitely attached to his mama, although their daughter was fast becoming a Daddy's girl, to even the score. Once she had her son in her arms, Jenny kissed his cheek and asked Daniel, "Is that it?"

He nodded, placed the box on the side table in the entryway, and ripped off the tape. He paused. "Do you want to do the honors?"

Her son drooled over the plastic car in his mouth, and she smiled. "You'd better. I know they won't be drool-free for long, but I need to try until I take some pictures to share with everyone."

Her son leaned against her chest, and she laid her cheek against the top of his head. "I love you, Cam, drool and all."

Daniel lifted the paper packaging away and raised the first book, flashing the front to her. The title, "An Introduction to Dragon-shifters: The Basics," was prominent, along with a shot of dragons flying in formation in the air.

The picture was of some of her clan members. MirrorPeak had been supportive of her, for the most part. And even now, she still worked on the few remaining skeptics, hoping to win them over.

She walked closer, as did her sister, and she said, "Open it, Daniel."

He did, slowly turning pages, the light hitting the glossy surface, and her eyes prickled with tears. "It's so pretty."

Her mate paused, lowered his head, and kissed her. "You're prettier."

She laughed. "Still the charmer."

Daniel winked, and she readjusted her hold on her son. "Put them somewhere safe until tonight."

Her sister spoke up. "I can watch the kids if you two want to go through them."

Jenny shook her head. "No, it's okay. Experiencing it with the clan at the upcoming celebration will be better. After all, I never would've been able to do this without their help."

It was true—the clan leader had liked her idea and convinced some of the clan members to help her with research and answering her questions.

Even the clan's children had helped, sharing what it was like to recently talk to their dragon for the first time.

She couldn't wait until her son and daughter experienced that for themselves.

Her son wiggled, and she could tell he wanted down. Placing him on the ground, he ran to his aunt and hugged her leg. "Auntie Jessie. Play with me."

Camden raised his car, and her sister smiled at him. "Only if I get to have the purple cars."

Her son scrunched his face. "The purple cars always win."

Jessica nodded. "You're right. So how about we both close our eyes and each pick two from the bin? That will be more fair, right?"

Camden bobbed his head. "Come on, Auntie. Let's play cars."

Her sister gently handed over Sofia, careful not to wake her, and took Camden upstairs to his bedroom.

Daniel immediately wrapped an arm around her shoulder and leaned down to kiss her cheek and then their daughter's. "Alone with my two females. How shall I spoil them this time?"

She laid her head against his shoulder. "Let's just enjoy this for a few moments. I love our children, but sometimes a few minutes of peace, in the arms of my mate, is pure heaven."

They both stared down at their daughter, content to be silent and take pleasure from each other's company.

Because even after years of Daniel cheating at games, his teasing, and his sometimes almost too protective attitude toward her and the children, she loved him more than ever before. On today of all days, when yet another dream of hers had come true, she needed to say, "I love you, Daniel."

He gently squeezed her shoulder. "I love you more."

As they looked at each other and smiled, Jenny debated arguing the point. However, he kissed her gently but thoroughly—so as to not wake the baby—and she forgot everything but her mate's taste.

She still felt like the luckiest woman in the world that he'd been the one to find her, back when she'd been stranded in the snow. And they were still just getting started on their happy ending.

Bonus Epilogue

Daniel Torres pulled the car up to the cabin, the very same one where he'd first taken Jenny after rescuing her from the cold, and his nearly nine-year-old son, Camden, immediately stated, "That's it? This is the special cabin where you and Mom met. It's super tiny."

He smiled. Even though his clan leader had offered to paint or pretty up the place—especially once they'd extended the borders of the clan and secured them against any potential threats—Daniel had declined. It still belonged to the clan, but every year, to celebrate when he'd met Jenny, he took his family here.

Oh, he had some private time with his mate to celebrate their actual mating ceremony date. But their very first meeting had been the beginning of their family's story, and he wanted everyone to enjoy it.

His six-year-old daughter Sofia bounced in her seat. "I like it, and the trees, and you said there's a stream nearby, Daddy?"

He turned off the ignition and turned in his seat. "Yes, little one. But we'll go tomorrow, when the sun isn't about to set."

His son sighed. "It'd be so much better to stay here in the summer. It's warmer, and the trees don't look dead, and more animals are around then."

Jenny—who was six months pregnant with their surprise third child—did her best to put some dominance in her voice, like Daniel had taught her. "What did we agree on before coming here?"

Her son groaned. "Not the contract."

Jenny nodded. "Yes, the contract."

Daniel struggled not to laugh at his son's overdramatic nature. His dragon spoke up. *I agree with Camden. It's stupid.*

He likes to find each and every loophole there is, so we have to put the terms on paper until he grows out of it.

His beast sniffed. *Still, summer would be a nicer time to visit.*

But it wouldn't be as special.

Since his dragon didn't want to argue, he curled up inside Daniel's mind and went to sleep.

Jenny's voice brought his attention back to the car. "MirrorPeak is nice enough to let us use this place, so we should be grateful. Besides, in the summer, they need to use it as a base for search and rescue operations."

Camden grumbled, "I suppose."

Daniel jumped in. "I don't know about you, but I want to go inside and build a fire. I might need some help."

His son sat up taller in his seat. "Let me help, Dad. I want to try and do it by myself. You said I'm old enough for that, and to try and chop a small piece of wood."

Sofia crossed her arms over her chest. "I want to do that too."

Camden shook his head. "You're still a baby, Sofia. You have to wait until you're grown up, like me."

"I'm not a baby!"

"Are too."

"Am not."

Camden pretended to rub his eyes and howl, like he supposedly thought babies behaved.

Sometimes it was hard not to laugh, but he most definitely couldn't or he'd never live it down.

So Daniel clapped his hands, and his children fell silent. "You know your mom hasn't been feeling too well, so let's be on our best behavior, okay?"

Both kids looked contrite. Every time she threw up, they worried—both the human and dragon halves.

Sofia murmured, "Sorry, Mommy."

Just as Camden said, "Sorry, Mom."

Jenny smiled and blew each of them a kiss. "No worries. Now, let's get inside. Sofia, you can help me get everything ready for s'mores while they build the fire." She lowered her voice dramatically. "We might even have to taste test each ingredient, just to make sure they're still good."

Sofia bounced in her seat. "Yes, Mommy. Let's do that!"

His son scowled, but didn't complain. It truly was a testament to how much he wanted to build a fire.

His dragon said sleepily, *He wants to impress you. So make a big deal of it.*

Since when are you the expert on children?

I listen to Jenny. She told me before to remind you.

He glanced at his mate, struggling to get up from her seat, and he placed a hand on her shoulder. "Wait, let me help you."

Daniel raced to the other side of the car, gently helped Jenny up, and wrapped her in his arms. "If we need to head back, just say so."

She shook her head. "No, no, I'm fine. This is going to be our last child, though, Daniel. I didn't have this much nausea or fatigue with the others. Plus, I didn't get this fat."

"You're not fat, you're perfect."

She snorted. "Even my swollen, mammoth-sized ankles?"

He tilted her head up and let his love shine in his gaze. "Every single inch of you. I wouldn't change a thing." He kissed her quickly before adding, "Well, except maybe your keen eyesight. Then I could finally cheat and win someday."

She laughed, lightly hit his chest, and replied, "No way in hell that's happening."

Camden giggled. "You said hell! You said hell!"

Jenny sighed, and Daniel somehow kept his face neutral. "Get inside and have everything ready to make a fire. Unless you want me to do it instead?"

His son dashed inside, still saying in a sing-song voice, "You said hell," and their daughter followed him, telling him to stop.

Once they were alone, Daniel cupped Jenny's cheek. "I love you." He kissed her, and then helped her inside. And after Camden got the fire going—all by himself—and they all roasted marshmallows for s'mores, Daniel couldn't help but smile at his little family. Their story had started in this cabin, and with each passing year, this place still added more memories and chapters to their lives.

And he couldn't ask for more.

Author's Note

I hope you enjoyed Daniel and Jenny's story! If you were a little surprised that they were the couple for Book 6 instead of Jon Bell and Cristina Juarez (the original couple planned for book #6), well, I realized at some point that Cris and Jon's story will probably be the final book in the entire series. Before figuring that out, I was sort of stumped as to what to write. Then it hit me—there were more stories ahead of theirs! So that's why it was pushed back.

The next story will be *The Dragon's Surprise* about the percentage-loving doctor, Kyle Baker, and a human female named Alexis. Let's just say she's going to throw his life into chaos, and it's going to be an awesome ride! Hopefully I can write it for 2024. And no, there's no preorder as of right now. :)

And now I have some people to thank for getting this out into the world:

- To all my beta readers—Sabrina , Iliana, and Ashley you do an amazing job at finding those lingering typos and minor inconsistencies.

And as always, a huge thank you to you, the reader, for

either enjoying my dragons for the first time, or for following me from my longer books to this series. Writing is the best job in the world and it's your support that makes it so I can keep doing it.

Until next time, happy reading!

About the Author

Jessie Donovan has sold over half a million books, has given away hundreds of thousands more to readers for free, and has even hit the *NY Times* and *USA Today* bestseller lists. She is best known for her dragon-shifter series, but also writes about magic users, aliens, and even has a crazy romantic comedy series set in Scotland. When not reading a book, attempting to tame her yard, or traipsing around some foreign country on a shoestring, she can often be found interacting with her readers on Facebook. She lives near Seattle, where, yes, it rains a lot but it also makes everything green.

Visit her website at: www.JessieDonovan.com